Lizzie McGuire

W9-CNL-574

Head Over Heels

Adapted by Jasmine Jones
Based on the series created by Terri Minsky
Part One is based on a teleplay written by Melissa Gould.
Part Two is based on a teleplay written by Douglas Tuber & Tim Maile.

Watch it on Disney Channel abc Kids

Disney Press
VOLO
New York

MADISON

Printed in the United States of America

First Edition
1 3 5 7 9 10 8 6 4 2

Library of Congress Catalog Card Number: 2003105747

ISBN 0-7868-4618-6
For more Disney Press fun, visit www.disneybooks.com
Visit DisneyChannel.com

Lizzie McGuire

PART ONE

CHAPTER ONE

"Okay," Lizzie McGuire said as she held up a tube of lilac-colored lip gloss. "This one says berry, but it tastes so much like vanilla. I love it anyway. Here—try it, Miranda."

Lizzie reached across her best friend David "Gordo" Gordon, who was propped at the Digital Bean counter reading a monster truck magazine, and handed the gloss to her other best friend Miranda Sanchez, who frowned at it, then unscrewed the top and gave it a sniff.

"Look, the Monster Truck Roundup is

coming to town!" Gordo said in a voice that was unnaturally excited, given that he was talking about big, loud cars. Gordo was generally more of a small, gas-efficient car kind of guy. "Six fun-filled hours of monster truck force and monster truck action!"

Lizzie looked at Gordo. What was his deal with monster trucks all of a sudden? Usually, the only monsters Gordo was interested in were the ones in 1950s-era black-and-white films—and that was only for artistic wise-crack-making purposes.

"What?" Gordo said. "I'm sick of talking about girl stuff." He scowled over at Miranda, who was busy applying the berry-vanilla lip gloss and smacking her lips together.

"Gordo, lip gloss is important," Lizzie protested. "By the way, since when have you been interested in monster trucks?"

"I'm a guy," Gordo said defensively. "And we never talk about guy stuff."

Lizzie looked over at Miranda, who was completely lost in Lip Gloss World. "Miranda?" Lizzie called.

Miranda snapped out of it, and smiled over at Lizzie. "Oh! Hi," she said, joining the conversation.

Gordo frowned. "Are you okay?"

"Yeah," Lizzie agreed, "you've been kind of quiet."

Miranda shook her head. "I don't know what's wrong with me. I can't eat. I can't sleep. I've been, like, totally distracted."

"Why?"

Miranda's eyebrows drew together. "I don't know. It all started in drama class yesterday when Ryan Adams did that monologue."

"Oh, yeah." Gordo nodded, remembering. "He was pretty good."

Miranda grimaced and shot Gordo the Look of Death. "Good?" she demanded. "*Good?* Ryan Adams wasn't good! He was *amazing*, Gordo." She raised her eyes to the ceiling and sighed. "Amazing!"

Lizzie thought back to drama class. Which one was Ryan again? Oh, yeah. He was that tall kid who did some weird monologue where he had to say all this totally bizarre-o stuff about "To be or not to be." Lizzie guessed it had been okay. She'd been kind of distracted by this hangnail that had been bothering her all day.

"And wasn't he cute, Lizzie?" Miranda gushed. "And smart. Really smart. And . . . what's that word?" Miranda wracked her brain. "Charismatic?" she guessed, then nodded. "He looked charismatic. I thought he was amazing, funny, and smart."

Lizzie grinned at her friend. "Oh, my

gosh," she said suddenly. "This is so exciting, Miranda!"

"I know!" Gordo agreed enthusiastically as he buried his nose back into his monster truck magazine. Where did that thing come from, anyway? Lizzie wondered. "*Nothing* says 'exciting' like the Monster Truck Roundup," Gordo added.

"Not that!" Lizzie protested. She pointed to where Miranda was grinning like a Cheshire cat in a pile of catnip. "This!"

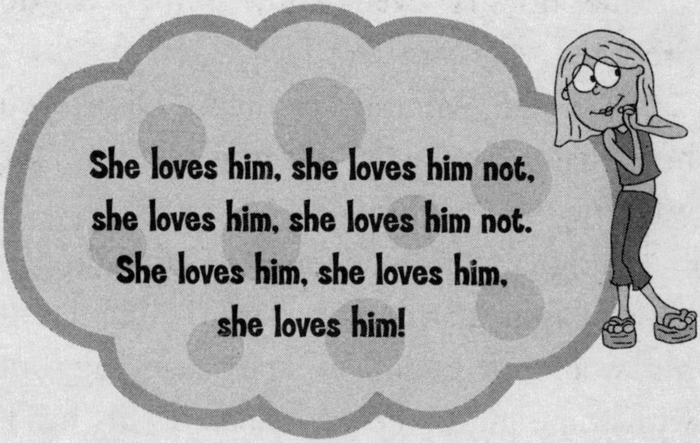
She loves him, she loves him not,
she loves him, she loves him not.
She loves him, she loves him,
she loves him!

"What?" Miranda asked.

"Miranda," Lizzie explained, "you're in love!" She nearly laughed out loud—it was so obvious! How could Miranda not see it?

Miranda looked completely confused. "I am?"

Gordo stared at Lizzie. "With who?"

Lizzie rolled her eyes. "With Ryan!" Sheesh, Lizzie thought. Am I the only one paying attention here?

Miranda touched her hair self-consciously. "Really?"

"She doesn't even know him!" Gordo protested.

"Yes I do!" Miranda insisted. "Didn't you hear that monologue? He was sensitive, he was cute, he was funny—"

"All right, all right, enough." Gordo flipped closed his magazine and hauled himself off his stool. "I've got to start hanging out with some guys," he said, shaking his head.

Gordo waved his hand dismissively in Lizzie's general direction and wandered out of the Digital Bean.

Miranda watched him go for a minute, scooted over, and took the seat Gordo had just left. "So, what do we do now?"

"Listen," Lizzie said, "as your friend, I'm going to do everything I can to get you two together."

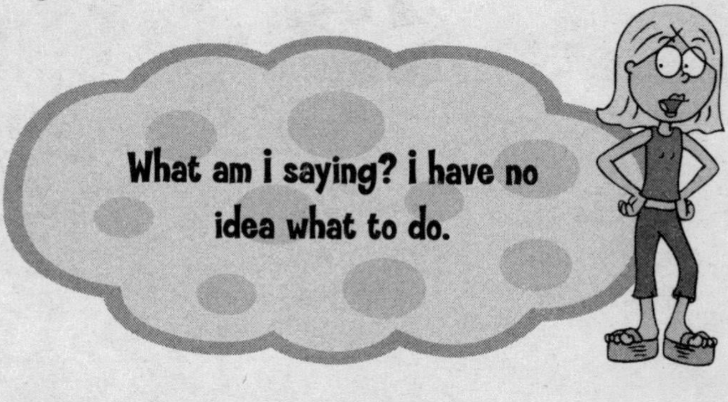

What am i saying? i have no idea what to do.

Lizzie looked into Miranda's glowing eyes and gulped. Okay, she thought, I just promised to help make Ryan Adams her boyfriend, and I have no clue how to do it.

Then again, Lizzie mused, that's never really stopped me before.

Sure, she thought, I can do this. After all, how hard can it be?

CHAPTER TWO

The next morning, Lizzie walked up to the counter in the kitchen where her annoying little brother, Matt, was already chowing down on a bowl of cereal. Lizzie reached for the box, and shook some of the wholesome wheat nuggets into her bowl. She frowned at the cereal, wondering why her mom wouldn't let her family have a box of Sugar-O's, like normal people.

Just as Lizzie lifted her spoon, she caught a

movement out of the corner of her eye. She looked over to where Matt was making a face that was even uglier than his usual one. "Mom!" Lizzie called. "Matt's staring at me."

Mrs. McGuire didn't even look up from the Rolodex she was flipping through. "Matt, stop staring at your sister," she said automatically.

Lizzie took another spoonful of cereal, but now Matt was making puking motions . . . and sound effects to go with them.

"What are you doing?" Mrs. McGuire demanded, looking at Matt.

"Clearing my throat," Matt said innocently. Then he launched into another round of vomit noises.

"Oh, Matt," Mrs. McGuire said, warningly.

Lizzie rolled her eyes. Did her mother seriously think that her I'm-so-disappointed-in-you voice was going to have any effect? Didn't she realize that only worked on Lizzie?

Mr. McGuire walked into the kitchen. "Morning, kids."

"Morning, Dad," Matt said brightly.

"Dad," Lizzie complained, "Matt won't let me eat my breakfast."

"Matt, let your sister eat her breakfast," Mr. McGuire said semi-sternly.

"But her face hurts," Matt protested.

"What?" Mr. McGuire looked over at Lizzie, worried.

Lizzie scowled at Matt. "What? My face doesn't hurt."

"I thought it did," Matt said seriously, then broke into a grin, "because it's killing me." He slapped the kitchen island and roared at his own joke.

Mrs. McGuire turned to her husband. "It's been going on all morning," she explained.

"All morning?" Mr. McGuire repeated. "Try their whole lives."

Lizzie narrowed her eyes at Matt. "What are you eating for breakfast?" she demanded. "A big bowl of ugly?" She shoved her cereal away and hopped off her stool. "I'm going to school."

"Ooh, I'll miss you," Matt said, batting his eyes at Lizzie. Then he rolled his eyes and snorted. "Not."

"Come on, you two," Mr. McGuire protested. "We're a family. We're supposed to like each other."

"But I *do* like Matt," Lizzie insisted. "I like it when he's not around. Later," she said as she stalked out of the kitchen.

Seriously, Lizzie thought as she grabbed her book bag, that's the best thing about school—I get to escape Matt for six whole hours. Compared to hanging out with my little brother, school looks like an island paradise. Especially now that I've got this cool new project to work on—the Miranda Love Project! I'm going for an A+.

"Ryan is totally the guy for me," Miranda said, breathlessly, as she and Lizzie stood in front of their lockers. "You're so smart to figure that out, Lizzie."

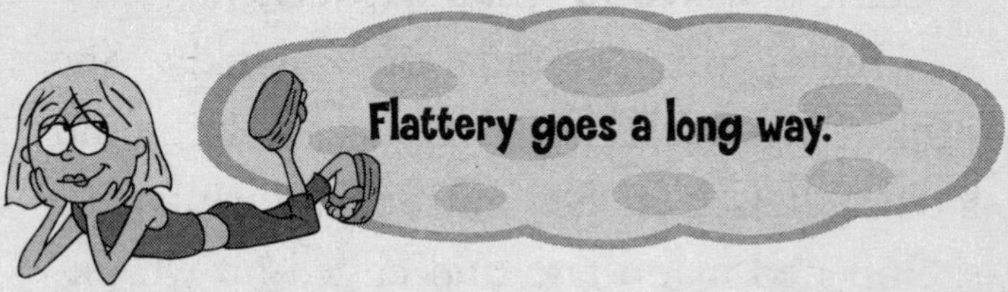
Flattery goes a long way.

"I mean, he's sensitive . . . he's funny. . . ." Miranda went on. "I mean, you could tell by the way he played that part, don't you think? I can't wait to tell him how good he was."

"Yeah," Lizzie agreed. "I'm sure he'll appreciate it."

"So how do I look?" Miranda asked, fiddling with her multicolored crocheted cap. "He should be walking by any minute. I usually see him between classes."

"Yeah, you look great," Lizzie said encouragingly. Then she bit her lip and added, "Except that you're sweating a little bit."

"I am?" Miranda asked in a panicky voice. "Where?"

Lizzie gestured to Miranda's locker.

"Oh, right," Miranda said quickly. She yanked the locker door open so she could look at herself in her mirror. Unfortunately, she opened it too fast, and ended up whacking Lizzie in the face.

"Ow!" Lizzie stumbled backward and slid to the floor in a heap.

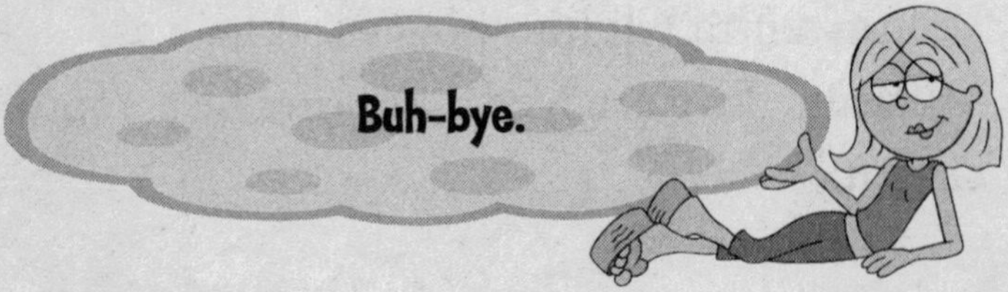

"Lizzie," Miranda cried, looking down at her friend, "are you okay?"

Lizzie nodded deliriously. Am I okay? she wondered. Well, except for the massive pain in my forehead and the horrible dizziness, I think I'm doing great. She held out her hand. "Oh, yeah, yeah, just help me up?"

Miranda reached for Lizzie's hand. "Sure."

"Ooh, there's Ryan!" Lizzie whispered fiercely as Miranda helped her struggle to her feet.

Miranda turned to look . . . and dropped Lizzie.

"Ow," Lizzie said as she dropped to the floor. *Again*, she added mentally.

But Miranda wasn't paying attention . . . she was on a mission. She stepped right in front of Ryan.

He smiled at her, a little uncertainly. "Hi," he said.

"Hi," Miranda said brightly. "Hi." Her mouth kept moving, and sounds were coming out, but they weren't making much sense. "I um . . . um . . . um . . ."

Lizzie stared at Miranda. What was going on? It wasn't like Miranda to get nervous around a guy. But Ryan didn't know that. Lizzie knew she had to do something, or Ryan would think that Miranda was a total freak! Lizzie struggled woozily to her feet.

Ryan frowned at Miranda. "Did you want to talk to me?"

"Uh," Miranda grunted. "I . . . uh . . . uh . . ."

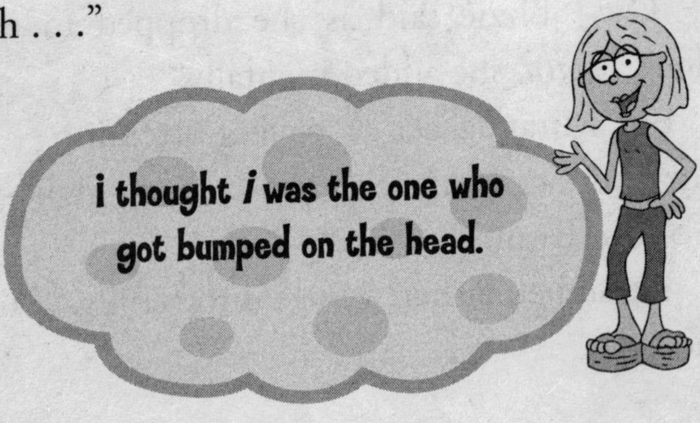

i thought *i* was the one who got bumped on the head.

"I . . . um . . ." Miranda went on.

Lizzie decided that this was as good a place as any to jump in. "Uh, yeah, she did," Lizzie said quickly. "We, we, uh, we saw you in the drama class yesterday. And she just wanted to tell you that you, uh . . . you were amazing. Amazing. Yeah!" Lizzie grabbed Miranda's arm. "She wanted to say that you were amazing."

"Amazing," Miranda said mechanically. "Ryan. Amazing."

Ryan grinned, revealing two dimples in his cheeks. "Thanks."

The dimples seemed to have a hypnotic effect on Miranda.

"So . . ." Ryan said uncomfortably. "Well, I guess, I'll see you guys later." He walked off down the hall.

"What is wrong with you?" Lizzie whispered fiercely to Miranda, once Ryan was out of earshot. "You couldn't even talk to him? You were totally freaking me out."

"*You're* freaked out?" Miranda demanded. "I just reminded myself of *you* just now!"

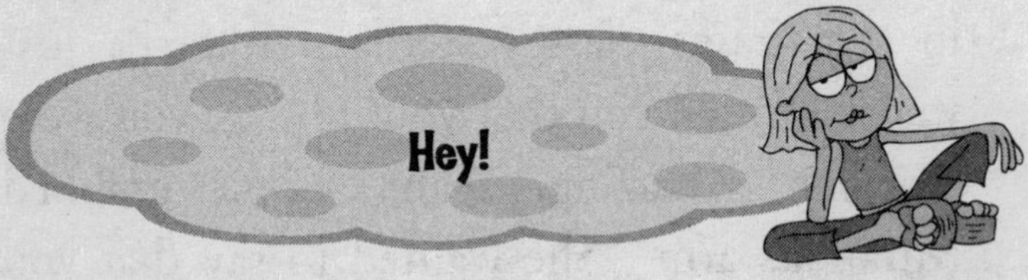

"This has never happened to me before," Miranda said, wide-eyed, as she and Lizzie started walking toward their next class. "What do I do?"

Lizzie shook her head. Honestly, she had no clue. How was Miranda supposed to get together with Ryan if she acted like a lobotomy patient whenever he was around? "Maybe you just got nervous," Lizzie said hopefully.

Miranda rolled her eyes. "Lizzie, this is me you're talking to," she said simply. "I don't get nervous. That's *you*."

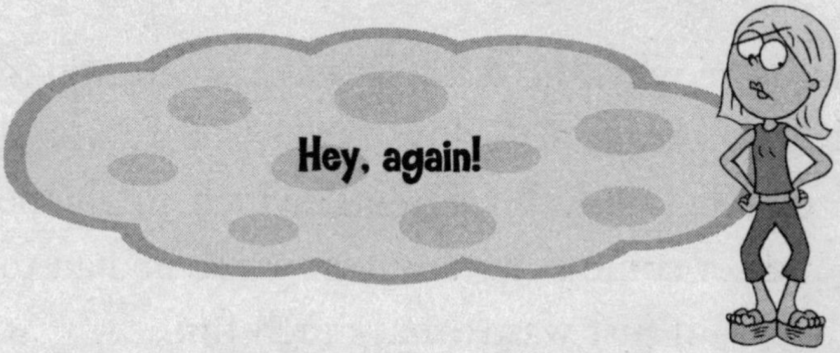

"Well, maybe you'll just have to try talking to him again," Lizzie suggested. "See what happens."

"I can't!" Miranda cried. "I choked! I stammered! I sweat!" She gestured wildly to herself. "I don't sweat!"

"Go!" Lizzie said, snapping her fingers at her friend. "Snap out of it!"

Miranda took a deep breath and shook her head. "This love stuff is freaky," she said.

Lizzie nodded. Tell me about it, she thought.

Matt was wearing his headphones and winding yarn around the deck furniture. He had no idea why. At least it was something to do . . . lame though it was. And it would probably annoy his parents, which might be good for some entertainment. Still, he had to admit—it just wasn't that much fun.

Gordo wandered out onto the deck. "Hey, Matt."

"I'm so bored," Matt complained.

"Where's Lanny?" Gordo asked.

"Quarantined," Matt explained as he kept winding the yarn around the furniture. "Highly contagious toe infection."

Gordo fell into step behind Matt. "What about Oscar?"

Matt shrugged. "His family wants him to stay away from me for a week," he said, still wrapping string around the furniture. "*He's* the one who wanted to see if his skin would prune if he stood out in the rain all day. I merely encouraged his curiosity."

"So did it prune?" Gordo asked.

Matt shook his head. "Nope."

Gordo looked around. "So where's Lizzie?"

"With Miranda," Matt said. He grimaced. "Talking about some boy."

Gordo groaned. Just once, he'd like to walk up to Miranda and Lizzie and find out that they were talking about baseball, or cars, or curly fries, or—or *anything* besides boys, makeup, and shopping.

"Here I am, thinking that eavesdropping on my sister would be fun," Matt said, "but my bad. It's so boring."

"I know," Gordo agreed as he pulled out his Hacky Sack. "Lizzie and Miranda are my best friends, but when they get into that 'boy' mode, there's, like, no talking to them."

"Personally, I don't get why you talk to them at all," Matt said.

"I just wish they were into the same stuff as

me," Gordo griped. "Like the Monster Truck Roundup."

He and Matt looked at each other. "It's coming to town, you know," they said at the same time.

Gordo cleared his throat. "Anyway . . ." He started kicking his Hacky Sack.

Matt watched Gordo keep his Hacky Sack airborne. "Say," he said after a minute, "how do you do that?"

"Here, it's easy," Gordo said. "Just watch." He gave the sack a few more kicks. "Sometimes I think my life would be so much easier if Lizzie were a guy."

"Yeah," Matt agreed. "I think my life would be easier if I had an older brother. You know, someone cool. Someone fun. Someone who could teach me stuff."

Gordo caught the sack, then held it out to Matt. "Here, you want to try?"

Matt pulled off his headphones and grabbed the sack. He gave it a kick that would have sent it across the backyard if Gordo hadn't grabbed it. "Hey!" Matt said suddenly.

Gordo looked at him. "What?"

"You and me. We could, you know, hang," Matt suggested.

Gordo pursed his lips, then shrugged. "Yeah, I guess," he said. "Sure, why not?"

Matt grinned. "I always knew you were too cool to be friends with my dorky sister."

CHAPTER THREE

"Okay," Lizzie said to Miranda, "let's have a practice conversation. I'm going to be Ryan, and you be you. Okay?"

Miranda frowned. "I guess." She was sitting on Lizzie's bed, looking a little down. She was clearly still weirded out by the fact that she couldn't even form a sentence when Ryan was around.

Lizzie walked over to her friend. "Okay." She cleared her throat and deepened her voice. "Hey, Miranda. I like your sweater." She punched Miranda lightly in the arm—guy style.

Miranda looked down at what she was wearing. "Uh, thanks, Lizzie," she said with a small smile. "But this is a T-shirt."

"Miranda," Lizzie wailed, "I'm *Ryan.*"

"Oh, right, right." Miranda nodded, and tried again. "Thanks, *Ryan.* How are you?"

"I'm doing good," Lizzie said in a swaggery boy voice. "You know, you should come to one of my plays sometime." She winked at Miranda.

Miranda struggled to suppress a giggle. "I'd love to."

"See?" Lizzie cried, dropping her boy persona. "That wasn't so hard."

"No," Miranda agreed. She rolled her eyes. "Just lame."

"Come on, Miranda," Lizzie protested. "At

least you were able to have a conversation with him."

Miranda laughed. "Yeah, because it was you!"

Lizzie sighed heavily. Why did I have to go and promise Miranda that I would help her get together with Ryan? She wondered. Being a good-deeder is so much work—especially when the good-deedee isn't cooperating, she added mentally as she looked at Miranda. Still, there has to be *something* we can do. . . .

Suddenly, Lizzie had a brainstorm, and pulled some index cards off her desk. She had been planning to use them for Spanish vocab flash cards, but whatever. This was way more important. "Okay," Lizzie said patiently, "we're going to make this real easy for you. We're going to write down everything that you have to say to Ryan. That way, next time you see him, you won't be so nervous. Okay?"

When i'm good,
i am really good.

Lizzie started scribbling some notes on the top card.

"But I'm no good at memorizing!" Miranda complained.

"So we'll make it short," Lizzie promised. "Don't worry. It'll be fine, okay?" She smiled encouragingly at Miranda.

Miranda smiled back gratefully. "Thanks," she said.

Lizzie nodded, then went back to her first flash card. "Ryan," she said aloud as she wrote. "How are you?"

See? Lizzie thought as she scribbled some more. How hard can it be?

CHAPTER FOUR

"So," Gordo said as he walked up to Lizzie, "where's your partner in crime?" He sat down across from her at the lunch table.

"Oh," Lizzie said in her most nonchalant voice, "Miranda's talking to Ryan."

"I thought she got all nervous and sweaty and tongue-tied around him," Gordo said.

"She did until I—" Suddenly, Lizzie remembered something. "Wait," she said slowly. "I thought you said you didn't want to hear any more 'girl talk.'"

"I don't, but since when do you listen to me?" Gordo wanted to know.

"I listen to you a lot," Lizzie insisted. "Oh, and—" she frowned, trying to remember what she was supposed to tell Gordo. The message hadn't made much sense. Especially since it came from Matt. Lizzie usually tuned out most of what he said. In fact, she had been so surprised that he was actually talking to her instead of insulting her that the message kind of went in one ear and out the other. "Matt told me to tell you that the Monster Truck Roundup has been postponed or something."

"Oh, no! It has?" Gordo's eyes were wide with disappointment.

Lizzie narrowed her eyes at him. "Are you, like, friends with my little brother now?" she asked. "'Cause I got to tell you, Gordo, that's kind of . . ." Lizzie searched for the right word. "Creepy."

"What can I say?" Gordo asked. "The kid's got spunk. It's refreshing."

He's got something, Lizzie agreed mentally. But I don't know if "refreshing" is the word I would use to describe it. Just then, Lizzie spotted Miranda. And she was walking onto the lunch patio with Ryan!

"Bye, Ryan," Miranda said happily. "See you tomorrow?"

Ryan grinned, nodding, then walked away.

Lizzie's eyes grew wide. "My gosh!" she said eagerly as Miranda walked over, grinning. "Tell me everything!"

"No, no, not *everything*," Gordo begged. "Please."

Miranda looked positively giddy. "Ryan said he wanted to have lunch with me tomorrow!"

"I knew writing down what to say would work!" Lizzie said happily.

Gordo stared at her. "You wrote down what she should say?"

Miranda blinked dreamily. "He said I have nice eyes!"

Lizzie squeaked. This was even better than she had planned!

Gordo was still gaping at Lizzie. "You wrote down what she should say?"

Miranda ignored Gordo. "And when I went on about his smile," she said to Lizzie, "he actually blushed!"

Gordo shook his head. "You wrote down what she should say?"

Lizzie rolled her eyes.

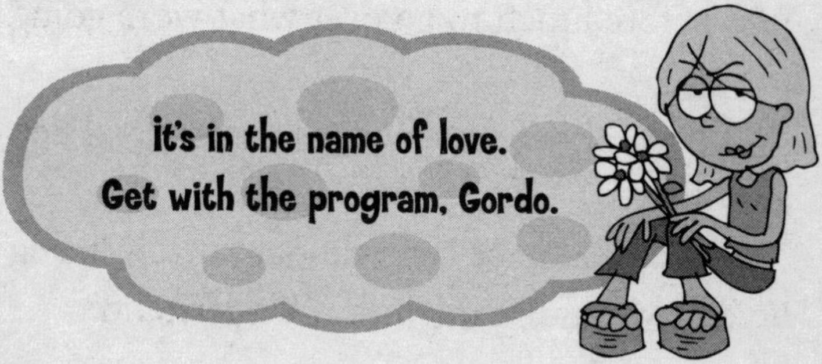

it's in the name of love.
Get with the program, Gordo.

"Yes, Gordo," Lizzie said, exasperated. "I wrote out a few words for Miranda to say to Ryan, okay? But look, now they have a date."

"That's . . . that's . . ." Gordo was dumbfounded. "Genius," he said finally.

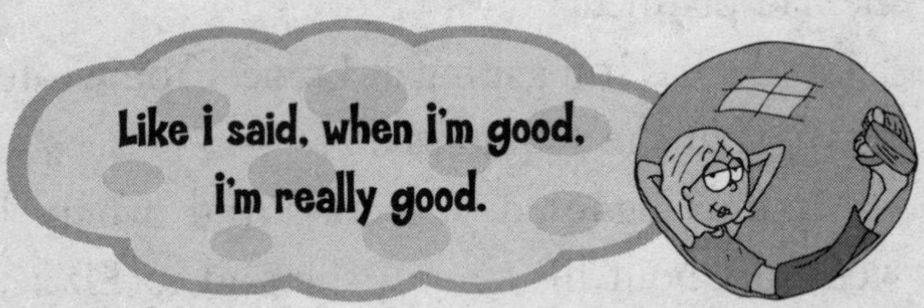

Like i said, when i'm good,
i'm really good.

"This is so awesome!" Lizzie said to Miranda.

"Thanks to you." Miranda looked utterly grateful. "Just meet me here a few minutes before lunch to go over what we're going to say."

"Okay." Lizzie reached for her soda. Then she blinked. "Wait, *what*?"

"I need you to be here without actually 'being here,'" Miranda explained. "Understand?"

Gordo nodded. "Finally, it gets interesting."

Lizzie hesitated. Somehow, this didn't seem like as good an idea as the flash card brainstorm had been. "I don't know, Miranda," she hedged.

"All you have to do is hide somewhere close." Miranda's dark eyes were pleading. "Listen to the way the conversation is going, and tell me what to say back to him. I won't be so nervous if you're here. Please?"

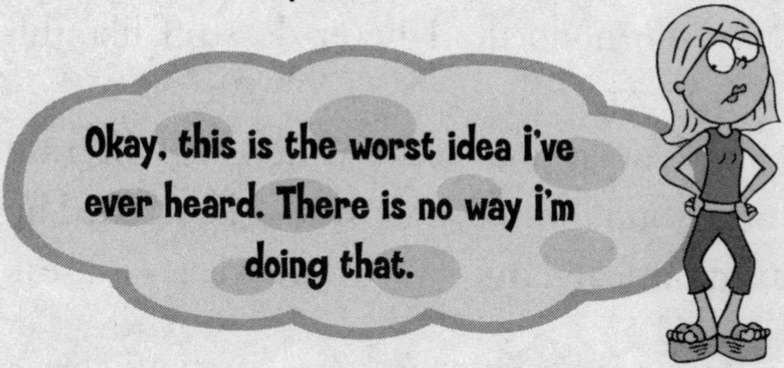

Okay, this is the worst idea I've ever heard. There is no way I'm doing that.

"So, you'll come, right?" Miranda begged.

Lizzie bit her lip. I should say no, she thought. I have to say no because this is a bad idea, and we're going to get caught, and it will never, ever work in a million, zillion years. But, in the end, she didn't say any of that. What she said was, "Yeah. Totally."

"He kicks!" Gordo shouted as he smacked the Hacky Sack with his foot. It sailed through the basketball hoop that was perched in the McGuires' backyard. "He scores!"

"That was awesome!" Matt cried. "We've got to invent games more often."

Gordo nodded. "I never do stuff like this with Lizzie."

"Of course not." Matt scoffed. "All this running around would make her"—he screwed up his mouth and put on a whiny voice—" 'break a nail.' "

"You got that right," Gordo said with a laugh.

Matt smiled. "I knew having an older

brother would rock!" he said warmly, then stopped. "I mean—"

"I know what you mean," Gordo said gently. "Come on, let's go get into some trouble."

Gordo threw his arm around Matt's shoulder, and they trotted out of the backyard to have some Guy Time. It was the most boy-centric day that Gordo had had in a long time. First, he and Matt took off on their scooters, hitting jumps and going at a breakneck pace. Lizzie and Miranda hated scooters. Lizzie refused to be seen on one ever since the first day she had tried it. She had started rolling and couldn't figure out how to stop and ended up smashing into the side of Mrs. Carver's minivan, which was parked at the end of the block. Gordo grinned. Now he had a scooter buddy—and could scooter around whenever he felt like it.

Gordo and Matt stopped for a monster truck magazine at a newsstand. Matt started flipping through the magazine and accidentally backed into a mean-looking motorcycle guy, who was parked at the curb. Lizzie and Miranda would have seen this guy and run for the hills, but he just looked at the magazine in Matt's hand and grinned. He, Matt, and Gordo gave one another a thumbs-up. This was some serious guy bonding.

After that, Matt and Gordo went back to the McGuires' backyard and invented a couple more games. Then they had a massive water fight with high-pressure water guns. Finally, they decided to toss the football around a little. Matt went long, and Gordo chucked it to him. Matt caught it, so Gordo decided to go for the field goal. Unfortunately, Gordo didn't have much practice with a football, so he ended up kicking it over the backyard fence and through the next-door-neighbor's window—*CRASH*—setting off the house alarm. Gordo and Matt looked at each other.

"Run!" Gordo shouted.

He and Matt took off and didn't stop running until they were three blocks away. Then they broke down laughing. Gordo couldn't stop—he could barely breathe, and tears were streaming down his cheeks. He couldn't believe that he had spent so much time with Lizzie and Miranda that he had actually forgotten how to kick a football. It was kind of sad, really.

Sad, yet hilarious.

He grinned at Matt, and Matt grinned back.

This guy stuff was definitely cool.

CHAPTER FIVE

Miranda sat at a table on the lunch patio, fiddling nervously with her hair. Ryan would be there at any minute, and she wanted to look good when he arrived.

"Ow!" Lizzie cried.

Miranda looked over to where her best friend was hiding in a trash can. Lizzie popped her head out of the can—the lid sat on her head like a sombrero—and rubbed her arm, grimacing. "I think I just got stung by something," Lizzie said.

"Lizzie!" Miranda whispered fiercely. "Get down before someone sees you!"

Lizzie crouched a little lower and scrunched up her nose in disgust. "You know it smells in here, Miranda, don't you?"

"That's what makes you such a good friend," Miranda said sweetly.

Grr. Oh, all right, Lizzie thought. As long as she realizes what I'm going through for her, I guess it's okay. . . .

"Ooh, here comes Ryan," Miranda said suddenly. She flashed Lizzie a hopeful smile. "My heart's depending on you."

"Hi, Miranda," Ryan said as he walked up to her table. "Thanks for having lunch with me."

Miranda looked at him and giggled nervously.

Lizzie rolled her eyes in disbelief. Her best friend couldn't even say hello without coaching? Lizzie had a sudden, horrifying image of herself, crouched in a trash can next to them on Miranda and Ryan's wedding day. Not pretty. Some kind of insect buzzed near Lizzie's ear. *Okay, let's do this fast so I can get out of here,* Lizzie thought. "Thanks for inviting me," she coached.

"Thanks for inviting me," Miranda echoed. Awkward silence.

"Please, sit," Lizzie prompted.

"Please, sit." Miranda gestured to the chair next to her.

Ryan smiled and sat down.

Suddenly, the buzzing near Lizzie's ear stopped. The bug—whatever it was—had landed on her neck. She swatted at it idly, and fierce pain burned at her collarbone. "Ow!" Lizzie cried.

"Ow!" Miranda repeated.

I can't believe that thing bit me again,

Lizzie thought. Weren't bugs supposed to *die* after they stung you? Wasn't that, like, a bug rule? Why was this one staying alive to sting her again? "Ooh, I think I just got stung again!"

"Ooh, I think I just got stung again!" Miranda echoed.

Lizzie stared at her friend. What was Miranda doing? Didn't she realize that this wasn't part of the plan?

At that moment, Miranda seemed to figure it out. Maybe because Ryan was staring at her as though she had just grown antennae. "I mean," Miranda said uncomfortably, "how *fun*. Again."

"Yeah," Ryan agreed. A warm smile appeared over his face. "This *is* fun."

Lizzie rubbed her shoulder. The only good thing about getting stung near the collarbone was that it almost completely took Lizzie's mind off the pain in her arm. She listened to the hideous silence that had settled between Miranda and Ryan and shuddered, but what could she do about it? I'm in too much pain to think of small talk, Lizzie thought.

"Oh, yeah," Miranda said to Ryan. She nodded, then sat in silence for another moment. "Can you hold on one second?" she asked suddenly. "I'm going to throw this. . . ." She picked up a napkin and nodded at it, then shoved her chair back and scurried over to Lizzie's trash can.

Miranda lifted the lid and tossed her napkin on Lizzie's head. "Quit fooling around, McGuire!" Miranda growled. "I need you!"

"I know, I know," Lizzie wailed, "but there's, like, a bee in here or something."

"Come on!" Miranda begged. Her face was panicky. "Ryan is waiting!"

Miranda scurried back to her seat by Ryan

as Lizzie wracked her brain for something to say. "Okay," Lizzie said, "uh, uh, you look nice."

"Oh, thank you," Miranda replied.

"Not you!" Lizzie said.

"Oh!" Miranda hurried back to Ryan. "You look nice, Ryan."

"Thanks," Ryan said. "So do you."

Lizzie's nose was tickling. Oh, no. A sneeze. She could just feel it coming on. Lizzie held her breath and tried to concentrate all of her will on not sneezing. One *achoo!* and it was all over—Lizzie's sneezes were notoriously loud.

Meanwhile, Miranda was unable to talk again. Lizzie had to help. "So, how are . . . ?" Lizzie began, then stopped. The sneeze was coming. She put her finger on her upper lip to stop it.

"So, how are . . . ?" Miranda began.

"How are . . . ?" Lizzie repeated.

"How are . . . ?" Miranda sat there, waiting for the rest of her line.

Oh, no, Lizzie thought. The sneeze was getting worse. "Ah . . . ah . . . ah . . ."

"Ah . . . ah . . . ah . . ." Miranda repeated faithfully. She stabbed at her lunch as though she wanted to kill it.

Ryan frowned. "Are you okay?" he asked Miranda.

Miranda giggled and nodded, but she couldn't think of a word to say. "Ah . . . ah . . . ah . . ."

Just then, the sneeze arrived in all of its glory. "*Ahhhhhhh . . . ccccchhhhhooooooo!*" Lizzie threw her head forward with the force of the sneeze. The trash can fell over, and Lizzie tumbled out . . . face-first.

Miranda gaped at her, then turned to Ryan and tried to fake a sneeze. *"Achoo,"* she said.

But Ryan was staring at Lizzie. "What are

you doing here?" he asked, frowning at Lizzie, who was still lying in a pile of garbage. "Why are you hiding in the trash can?"

"I . . . I . . ." Lizzie looked from Ryan to Miranda. You explain, Lizzie thought.

But clearly Miranda didn't get the mental message. "Yeah, Lizzie," Miranda demanded. "What *are* you doing here?"

"No," Lizzie said as she struggled to her feet. "I can explain."

Ryan looked from Lizzie to Miranda and back again, completely confused. "Yeah, well . . ." he said uncomfortably. "I've kind of got this thing . . . I'll see you later, Miranda." He grabbed his lunch bag and hurried away.

He's afraid of us, Lizzie thought as she watched Ryan's hasty retreat. And who can blame him? *I'm* kind of afraid of us right now.

"He hates me!" Miranda wailed. "He hates

me! He'll never speak to me again! We'll never go on a second date, I'll never get a first kiss or . . . or . . ." Her eyes grew wide with horror. "A wedding!"

Well, at least I won't have to wear a garbage can as a bridesmaid's dress, Lizzie thought, then caught herself. No—this was *not* over. She wasn't about to give up on her promise to Miranda that easily. "Come on, Miranda," Lizzie said reasonably. "All you have to do is go talk to him and tell him the truth, okay? It's going to be fine. It's not a big deal."

"I can't, Lizzie!" Miranda said. "I can't be near him—bad things happen." Miranda shook her head, blinking back tears. "I've got to go."

Lizzie sighed as she watched her friend hurry away.

This is my fault, Lizzie thought guiltily. I knew this trash can idea would never work—

I shouldn't have agreed to do it. I messed everything up, and now I have to fix it . . . for Miranda.

But first, I have to get myself out of this garbage can.

CHAPTER SIX

"Oh, hey, Gordo," Lizzie said as she looked up from her homework. She had been sitting on the living room couch, struggling with algebra for the past half hour. "I thought you left after dinner."

"I tried, but then Matt challenged me to a game of hacky-basket." Gordo leaned against the couch arm and folded his arms across his chest. "That kid never tires, does he?"

Lizzie bit her lip. She really couldn't think about her little brother right now. She had much bigger problems. "Have you talked to Miranda?" Lizzie asked. "She's not answering her phone."

Gordo's eyebrows drew together. "Guess she's still upset about that whole thing with Ryan." He shook his head suddenly. "Doh! Why can't I stop talking about that stuff?"

"I was just trying to help, and now she's all angry at me," Lizzie said miserably.

"Well, why don't you try talking to Ryan?" Gordo suggested. "Tell him what happened." He shook his head again and sighed. "There I go again. It's like a disease!"

"Maybe I should try that," Lizzie said, doodling in her notebook. She always doodled when she was thinking hard. "I could talk to Ryan. That's a great idea."

"Hey, Gordo," Matt said as he trotted into the living room. "I found this Web site, and it's all about cheese."

Gordo smiled. "Sorry, little man, but I've got to get going."

"How 'bout another round of hacky-basket, then?" Matt asked eagerly.

Gordo looked at Matt. Lizzie had to bite back a chuckle. Clearly, Gordo was all hacked out.

"Matt," Gordo said slowly, "do you remember when I was talking to you about responsibility?"

Matt shook his head. "Not really."

"I got to go," Gordo explained. "I've got homework to do. And I've got to pair up my socks." He looked down toward his feet sadly. "They never seem to match anymore."

"See—that's what happens when you start hanging with MC Dorkalot," Lizzie put in. "You, too, become a dork."

"You're one to talk, Lil' *Dim*," Matt snapped back.

Gordo laughed, and Matt looked up at him, excited. "If you don't want to play hacky-basket, I'll show you the Web site. It's about *cheese.* A guy actually built a house out of it."

Lizzie rolled her eyes. "Wow," she said sarcastically. "Cheese house. How cool."

"Wait a second," Gordo said with a frown. "A guy built a house? Out of cheese?" He blinked. "What kind of cheese?"

Lizzie gaped at him. Was Gordo actually serious? He thought some cottage made out of Velveeta bricks was, like, interesting? "Gordo," Lizzie explained, "I was being sarcastic."

"They have pictures," Matt singsonged temptingly.

Lizzie winced at the mental image of some overweight guy standing next to his Gouda palace. Gross.

Gordo glanced at Lizzie, then turned to Matt. "Well, I guess my homework's going to have to wait."

"Yes!" Matt cried.

Lizzie shook her head as Gordo and Matt scampered out of the room to use the computer. Boys can be so strange, Lizzie thought.

CHAPTER SEVEN

Lizzie spotted Ryan in the hall the next morning. It was now or never. Miranda's heart is still counting on you, she told herself, remember? She squared her shoulders and strode over to Ryan. "Look, Ryan," she said firmly, "we need to talk."

"Yeah," Ryan agreed, nodding, "we do."

Lizzie launched into her explanation. "Look, the whole reason I was telling Miranda what to—"

"You don't need to explain," Ryan said gently.

Lizzie stopped, surprised. "I don't?"

"Nope." Ryan put his arm around Lizzie and pulled her into step next to him, so that they were walking down the hall together. "I totally get it."

Lizzie smiled with relief. "You do?"

"Don't be shy around me, Lizzie," Ryan said smoothly. "I like you."

Wait a minute, Lizzie thought. Something about this conversation was definitely off. "What?"

"I think it's cute you had Miranda do all the talking for you," Ryan assured her.

Oh, no. This was getting totally messed up!

"Uh, you've got this all backward, Ryan," Lizzie said quickly. "See, what we were doing—" Just then, the bell for first period rang. Lizzie tried to shout over the deafening noise—Ryan *had* to hear this *right away.* "I was just hiding in the trash can, telling

Miranda what to say because she gets so nervous around you, Ryan. She really likes you," Lizzie explained. The bell finally stopped ringing. Whew. Lizzie thought. At least now I can hear myself think. But Ryan was still looking at her, confusion stamped across his face. "And that's all we were doing," Lizzie finished. She frowned at Ryan's hand, which was planted on her shoulder.

"Look," Ryan replied, "I couldn't quite hear everything you said. Let's pick this up later, okay? The Digital Bean, after school?" He dropped his arm from her shoulder and turned away. "Later."

"No," Lizzie protested, "I'm not—" But Ryan had already drifted off down the hall. *Grr.* This had not gone according to plan. Lizzie turned to head to her first class, and came face-to-face with Miranda . . . who looked stunned—and hurt.

"Miranda!" Lizzie cried in surprise. "You are *never* going to believe what just happened."

"How could you do this to me?" Miranda asked.

"What are you talking about?" Lizzie demanded. "Do what? I was just explaining to Ryan everything that was going on."

"Oh, yeah," Miranda said sarcastically. There was a catch in her voice, and she had to blink back tears. "That's why Ryan just asked you out?"

Lizzie shook her head. That wasn't what had happened at all. Was it? "Miranda, you don't—"

"Save it, Lizzie," Miranda told her. "You've said enough."

Miranda stormed off, leaving Lizzie standing alone. Okay, this was not the plan, Lizzie thought miserably. This was definitely *not* the plan!

CHAPTER EIGHT

Gordo kicked the Hacky Sack through the basketball hoop for the four hundred and fifty-first time that day. He'd done it so much that it wasn't even challenging anymore. But Matt still got excited every single time Gordo made it.

"Oh, yes!" Matt shouted as Gordo's shot went in. "Okay, four out of five, winner gets to short-sheet Lizzie's bed."

"Matt, we've been playing this game

for five hours." Gordo groaned, exhausted.

Matt chucked the Hacky Sack through the basket. "And my bedtime's not for another three."

Gordo sighed. "Look," he said, "we need to have a talk. I know you're going to find this hard to believe, but I miss Lizzie. Miranda, too."

"Hey!" Matt said brightly, ignoring what Gordo had just said. "You know what? We can glue Lizzie's favorite chips together. That way, when she goes to open the bag, they'll come out in one big clump." He let out an evil laugh.

"But you've already put peanut butter in her shoes—" Gordo protested.

Matt planted his hands at his waist. "Actually, it was jelly. But I'll remember the peanut butter for next time."

Gordo sighed. He knew that there was no

getting around it—it was time for the Big Talk. "You know, Matt, we've had a lot of fun these past couple of days," Gordo began.

"Tons of fun," Matt agreed.

"The hanging out . . ." Gordo listed. "The hacky-basket. Cheese house. But truth is, I really need to start hanging out with Lizzie again."

"That's crazy talk," Matt insisted. "Come on, let's go see if there's anything of Lizzie's lying around we can destroy."

"Sorry, little buddy." Gordo shook his head. "No can do. She's one of my best friends. And believe it or not, she and I have a lot in common."

"But she's so boring!" Matt wailed.

"Look," Gordo said gently. He really didn't want to hurt Matt's feelings, but he knew that if he played another game of hacky-basket, he would go totally berserk. "You're just a kid.

You have plenty of time to do stuff before *you* become boring. Invent another game. Learn to juggle. Build your very own cheese house."

Matt grinned. "Hey. Now you're talking."

Gordo nodded. "Well, I'm going to go now. But we can still hang out on occasion."

"Really?" Matt asked eagerly. "When?"

"Whenever."

"Tomorrow?" Matt suggested.

Gordo winced and shook his head. "Mmm, no."

Matt tried again. "This weekend?"

Gordo sighed. Matt sure wasn't making this easy. "Mmm, no," Gordo said softly. "How 'bout the next time the Monster Truck Roundup's in town?"

Matt thought about this for a minute, then grinned. "Cool," he said.

Gordo grinned back. He had to admit—having a "kid brother" was kind of cool . . .

sometimes. Gordo was just glad that he didn't have to have one permanently . . . like Lizzie did.

Lizzie dragged Miranda into the Digital Bean. *Number one, I am not going on this "date" alone,* Lizzie thought as she pulled Miranda by the hand. *Number two, it's time to end this thing once and for all. I'm not hiding in any more garbage!*

Miranda spotted Ryan and yanked her hand away from Lizzie. "I don't need to be here," she snapped.

"Yes, you do!" Lizzie insisted.

Ryan smiled at Lizzie and Miranda. "Good, you made it," Ryan said. "I got us a table, Lizzie." He grabbed Lizzie's arm.

Lizzie rolled her eyes, shrugging off Ryan.

"Bye," Miranda said, turning to go.

Lizzie grabbed her arm. Miranda wasn't

getting away that easily. "Miranda, wait," Lizzie insisted.

"Lizzie, it's okay," Ryan said kindly as the three of them grabbed their seats. "Like I told you before, you don't have to be so shy around me. Miranda doesn't have to do the talking for you."

Okay, that's it! Gloves are coming off, walls are coming down! i'll show you who's shy!

"Ryan," Lizzie said firmly, "look—"

"Wait," Miranda interrupted. "What did you say?"

"Ryan, look . . . ?" Lizzie repeated.

Miranda laughed. "Not you," she said to Lizzie. She turned to Ryan. "You."

"I said you don't have to do the talking for

Lizzie anymore," Ryan explained. "I'm sure she'll find her voice, now that everything's out in the open."

Miranda gaped at him. "Wait a sec," she said. "In the monologue, you were so much smarter than this. So insightful and sensitive."

"Ah," Ryan said knowingly. "The curse of the good actor."

Lizzie and Miranda stared at him. The what? Lizzie wondered.

"People don't see you," Ryan explained. "They only see the person you're playing."

Miranda looked at Lizzie, then at Ryan. "You know what?" she said slowly. "I think that's been my problem. I didn't fall for you. I fell for the guy you were playing."

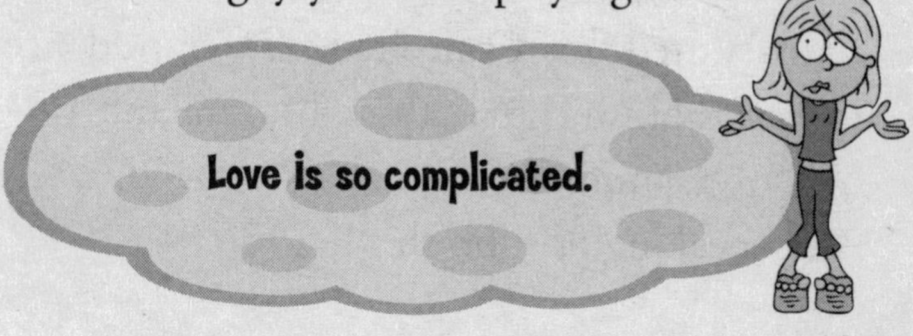
Love is so complicated.

"Wait a minute," Ryan said, staring at Miranda as though he had just really realized that she was there. "*You're* the one that likes me?"

Miranda cocked an eyebrow. "Let's make that *liked*." She shook her head. "You know what? Now that I think about it, that whole crush thing doesn't even work for me. I get all jittery and sweaty all the time." She curled her lip. "Who wants *that*?"

"Well, I'm sorry you feel that way," Ryan replied, "but, you know, I'm happy to give you an autograph." He smiled and took a sip of his smoothie.

Miranda let out a snort of laughter and stood up. "Later."

She and Lizzie walked away from Ryan the Dim-Witted Yet Conceited. Good riddance to bad rubbish, Lizzie thought, remembering one of Gammy McGuire's favorite phrases. And speaking of rubbish . . .

"Hey, Miranda," she said, grabbing her best friend's arm, "can you make up your mind if you like someone *before* I climb in a garbage can?" Lizzie smiled at her best friend.

Miranda laughed. "Sorry," she said sincerely. "And by the way, even if Ryan were the guy for me, I should've never let him come between us. I'm sorry." She put her head on Lizzie's shoulder.

"It's okay," Lizzie promised. "We're friends. Even if we get in a fight and you walk away from me, you'll always know where to find me. Okay? Right here." She grinned. "Let's go find Gordo."

Miranda nodded. "Oh, yeah."

Lizzie was glad that this whole experiment in crushdom was over. It hadn't been as much fun as she had thought that it would be. Besides, she missed Gordo. Maybe we could talk about some guy things once in a while,

Lizzie mused. Then she got a grip. Naah—what am I thinking?

"I can't believe that after all that drama, your crush on Ryan is actually over," Gordo said later that night as he stared up at the stars over the McGuires' backyard.

"I can't believe you're still talking about it," Miranda snapped back.

"He's making up for lost time," Lizzie joked.

But Gordo didn't take the bait. "I guess," he said slowly, as though he were lost in thought. "Let's just say, you two guys aren't half as bad as the stuff you talk about constantly." He nodded. "It's good to be back."

Lizzie sat up and brushed the grass off her clothes. "So, anyone hungry?" she asked as she hauled herself to her feet.

"Me," Miranda said quickly, hopping up.

Gordo stood up with them. "Me, too."

"There's some chips in the kitchen," Lizzie said, heading toward the back door. "Let's go."

"I don't think you want to eat the chips," Gordo said.

"Why not?" Lizzie asked.

Gordo opened his mouth to reply, then seemed to think better of it. "Never mind," he said.

Lizzie shrugged, wondering what Gordo was talking about. Then she thought about Ryan. *What a freakish mystery his mind turned out to be,* Lizzie thought. *Boys. Who could figure them out? Maybe everything will make sense one day,* she supposed. *Like, when I'm older, and in high school and stuff.*

Lizzie pulled down the bag of chips and poured them into a bowl. They came out in a massive clump. Lizzie stared at them. Someone had actually *glued* them together!

And then again, Lizzie thought, as she watched Gordo giggle his head off, maybe boys will never make sense. . . .

Lizzie looked over at Miranda, who was rolling her eyes and shaking her head. Lizzie sighed with relief . . . but at least I have Miranda to help me try to figure them out.

PART TWO

CHAPTER ONE

"Did you know that there was cannibalism in Trinidad and Tobago until 1850?" Lizzie McGuire's best friend David "Gordo" Gordon asked as he sat propped on the windowsill of Hillridge Junior High's Webzine office. Lizzie narrowed her eyes at him, then turned back to her computer monitor, trying to concentrate on the article she was writing. And no, she wasn't writing about cannibals. The bits of information Gordo was feeding her were just part of his idea of what it meant to be helpful—to stand there and spew random, disgusting facts while she was trying to work. If Lizzie tried to interrupt Gordo's monologue of revolting trivia, he would just look hurt. Of course, if *she* ever tried to give him some helpful fashion advice while he was doing his math homework—forget it. Gordo would freak.

"There were a lot of pirates in that area, too," Gordo went on. "They liked to drag their prisoners under their ship across the razor-sharp coral reefs. On the other hand, they invented barbecue food. Are you hungry?" He rubbed his stomach. "I'm hungry."

Lizzie frowned. Is he serious? she wondered, trying to suppress her annoyance. Could Gordo really be hungry after spending half an hour tossing barf-inducing factoids at her?

"Gordo?" Lizzie said, nodding at her

computer monitor. "I'm trying to finish my article in time for this week's edition."

Gordo leaned over and looked at her headline. "'School to Schedule Weekly Movie Night,'" he read aloud. For a minute, Lizzie thought that seeing the headline might actually make Gordo realize that she was trying to get some work done, but instead it just sent him off down another branch of the trivia tree. "Did you know that motion pictures weren't really invented by Edison, like everybody thinks?" Gordo asked. "They were invented by William Friese-Greene, but he needed money, so he sold the patent to Edison. Edison was almost completely deaf. And he had eyebrows like out to *here*," Gordo said as he gestured to a place about a foot in front of his face.

"Gordo!" Lizzie wailed.

Gordo winced. "Sorry," he said. "I'll zip it."

Lizzie started typing again, and Gordo leaned back in to look at her article.

"Wow, they're showing *The Mummy*?" he asked, clearly excited.

Lizzie sighed impatiently. "Fine, Gordo," she snapped, "what do you need to tell me about *The Mummy*?"

Gordo stared at her, wide-eyed. The Innocent Act, Lizzie thought. Ah, I know it well.

"Um, that I enjoyed it?" Gordo said.

Lizzie lifted her eyebrows. "Is that all?" she demanded.

Gordo nodded, and Lizzie turned back to her monitor and started keyboarding again.

"And when they made mummies, they used to pull their organs out through their nose," Gordo added.

Lizzie rolled her eyes. She should have known that nothing could stop the tide of

Gordo's Puketastic Triviathon. Lizzie clicked SAVE and popped the disk out of her computer, then pushed her chair back, glared at Gordo, and walked up to the front of the Webzine office, where the journalism teacher, Mr. Lang, was busy working on a book of crossword puzzles.

"Here's the movie night story, Mr. Lang," Lizzie said brightly, placing the disk on his desk. Lizzie folded her arms across her chest and went on. "I feel like I've got a real handle on this journalism stuff. I think the story lead's a real grabber."

Mr. Lang didn't look up.

Lizzie took a deep breath and plunged ahead. "So. For my next story, I was thinking I could do the school play. Mr. Escobar, the drama teacher, wrote it."

Mr. Lang still didn't say anything and still didn't look up from his book. He did blink, though, and Lizzie decided to take this as a good sign. "My best friend Miranda is auditioning for it," Lizzie babbled. Miranda Sanchez was Lizzie's other best friend. "She'll probably just get a small part, so I think I can cover that all the way from auditions to opening night."

"Bermuda!" Mr. Lang shouted.

Lizzie stared at him a moment, unsure how to respond. She had thought of many things that Mr. Lang might say about her story idea, but "Bermuda!" was so not on the list. "I, uh, beg your pardon?" Lizzie asked.

"Seven-letter word for 'putting surface,'" Mr. Lang explained as he scribbled the letters into the crossword boxes.

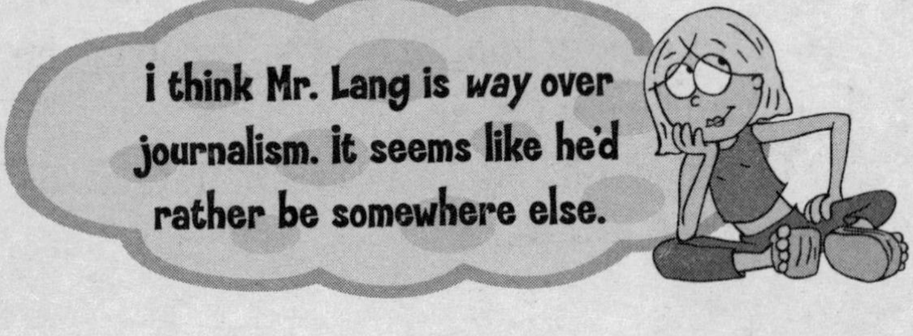

i think Mr. Lang is *way* over journalism. it seems like he'd rather be somewhere else.

Lizzie looked down at Mr. Lang, who sat busily involved in his crossword puzzle book. She had to admit, Mr. Lang's life didn't look too glamorous. She was sure he'd rather be behind the wheel of a sports car, surrounded by supermodels with big hair. Or maybe zooming across blue waters on a pair of water skis . . . surrounded by supermodels with big hair. Or even planting a flag on the moon . . . surrounded by supermodels with big hair. Lizzie guessed that hair could get really big in zero gravity. *I guess I shouldn't be so hard on the guy for wishing he was somewhere else,* she thought. *In fact, I'm beginning to feel that way myself.*

"So, I'll do the story on the play, then," Lizzie said, snapping out of her reverie.

No answer. Mr. Lang stared down at his crossword. He was in deep thought about 35 across.

"And I'll have it for you after opening

night," Lizzie promised, although she wasn't sure why she was bothering. She walked out from behind Mr. Lang's desk and ticked off her plans on her fingers. "There'll be a review, details on the production. . . ." Lizzie cleared her throat. "Well, it'll just be all about the play." She giggled nervously. This was going nowhere. She glanced over at Gordo—after all, he never had any trouble thinking of things to say. Maybe he knew some fascinating tidbits about Bermuda, or something. "Gordo?" Lizzie squeaked. "A little help here?"

"Well, apparently the Egyptians had this wooden hook that went right into the nose. . . ." Gordo began.

Lizzie sighed. This was going to be a long afternoon.

"You know," Gordo said, "when you become a famous reporter, I can come along and take all the pictures. Photographers get to wear stuff with lots of pockets." He stared off into space, probably picturing the pockets. "I like that," he said.

Lizzie rolled her eyes. It was a few days later, and she was eating lunch in her usual spot, across from Gordo in the cafeteria. Everything was business as usual—Lizzie had her same old peanut-butter-and-banana sandwich, Gordo had his usual chocolate milk, and Larry Tudgeman, the school nerd, had just exited the lunch line with a plateful of Broccoli Surprise. "I don't think you'll be my photographer, Gordo," Lizzie said. "I don't plan on doing any fashion shows or swimsuit competitions."

"Oh." Gordo looked disappointed. "Forget it, then."

Just then, Miranda ran into the cafeteria. "Omigosh!" she squealed as she barreled toward Lizzie and Gordo, slamming into

Tudgeman. Broccoli bits flew everywhere.

"Oh, I'm sorry, Tudgeman!" Miranda called to Larry, who had already bent over to gather his lost broccoli. Miranda slid into the seat across from Lizzie. "I . . . I got it! I didn't even try to, but I got it!"

"What did you get?" Lizzie asked eagerly. "What did you get?"

"The lead in the play!" Miranda cried, grinning like crazy. "I'm going to be the star of the school play!" She shook her fists in excitement.

Lizzie gasped. "Oh, that is so awesome! Congratulations."

"I thought I'd get in the chorus or paint scenery or something," Miranda went on, "but, no, I got the biggest part!"

"That is so great," Lizzie said. "I didn't know you were such a good actress."

Miranda shrugged. "To be honest, I didn't have any real competition. Mr. Escobar wrote the play himself, and it's set in the 1950s, which is, like, a million years ago." Miranda waved her hand as though she were shooing away a prehistoric bug. "And none of the regular drama kids wanted to do it. They all wanted to do something where they were supermodels and NBA stars who turn into crime-fighting, rapping robots."

"Now, *that's* a great idea," Gordo said with a grin.

Lizzie gave him a playful swat. "But still," Lizzie said to Miranda loyally, "you're the star of the play! You got the biggest part." She smiled. "None of us has ever even been in a play before."

"*I* have," Gordo volunteered.

Lizzie and Miranda stared at him.

"In the third-grade grammar pageant," Gordo explained. "I played the Question Mark."

Lizzie had to bite her lip to keep from

laughing. It was just too easy to picture little Gordo as a giant punctuation mark.

"Gordo?" Lizzie said. "That might not help you get dates."

Gordo shrugged and turned to Miranda. "Okay, but if you guys ever need help looking confused, inquisitive, or questioning, I'm your guy." He drew his eyebrows together and frowned. Then he rubbed his chin, as though he were concentrating. Then he scratched his head.

Is Gordo trying to look curious, or like he's got a horrible case of dandruff? Lizzie wondered. Either way, she was glad that Miranda was the actor and not Gordo, whose training as a question mark was definitely, uh . . . questionable.

This is going to be so great! Lizzie thought. *Miranda has the lead in the school play, and I'm going to write about it.*

CHAPTER TWO

"Hey, Matt," Mr. McGuire said as Lizzie's little brother walked into the kitchen with his silent partner, Lanny. Mr. McGuire nodded at Matt's friend. "Lanny, how're you doing? What've you been up to?" Mr. McGuire peered at the contents of a big green pot while Mrs. McGuire stirred something that was bubbling away in a saucepan on the burner next to his.

Matt sat down on a stool and looked at his

parents with a prim little smile. Lanny sat down next to Matt and blinked.

"Why do you bother?" Mrs. McGuire whispered to her husband. "You know he's not going to say anything."

"I'm going to get something out of him," Mr. McGuire muttered stubbornly. "Watch." He cleared his throat and turned to Lanny. "So, Lanny," Mr. McGuire said brightly, "you want to stick around for dinner? 'Cause we're having Gammy McGuire spareribs." Gammy McGuire was Lizzie and Matt's grandmother.

"He can't," Matt said quickly. "He has church choir practice tonight."

Mr. and Mrs. McGuire looked at each other. Choir? They had never even seen Lanny move his lips.

"Besides," Matt went on, "ribs give Lanny nightmares." Matt looked at Lanny. "The walrus dream, right?"

Lanny looked down at the floor, as though he didn't want to talk about it. Not that he would have said word one about it, anyway.

"Right," Matt went on. "Hey, Mom, can I have three thousand dollars for a Jet Ski?" He grinned.

"Well, no," Mrs. McGuire said.

"Could I have one thousand dollars for an electronic keyboard?" Matt tried again.

"I don't think so," Mr. McGuire snapped.

Matt sighed. "All right," he said in his best Gee-I'm-so-disappointed voice. "I guess I'll just settle for ninety dollars for walkie-talkies."

Mrs. McGuire looked at Matt over the tops of her glasses. "Matt, we are not giving you ninety dollars."

Matt frowned and turned to his friend accusingly. "See, Lanny?" Matt demanded. "I told you they wouldn't fall for the start-high-go-low thing."

Lanny clenched his fists and shook them in frustration.

"What do you need walkie-talkies for, anyway?" Mr. McGuire asked.

"So me and Lanny can talk to each other at night and when we're on our way to school and stuff," Matt explained.

"You know, your mom and I aren't here just to give you money, Matt," Mr. McGuire said in a warning tone.

"I know you're not just here to give me money," Matt chirped. "You have to cook and wash my clothes and do all that stuff, too."

"What your father is trying to say," Mrs. McGuire explained as patiently as possible, "is that we work hard for our money, so if you want expensive things, you have to earn them."

"That's right, sport," Mr. McGuire chimed in. "If you want those walkie-talkies, you're just going to have to get out there and earn the money yourself."

Matt's eyebrows drew together in confusion. *"Why?"* He looked over at Lanny, who shrugged. Matt often felt that his parents made no sense, but he knew better than to argue. Instead, Matt and Lanny trudged into the living room and started rooting around in the sofa cushions for loose change.

"Earn it yourself?" Matt grumbled. His voice was slightly muffled because his head was buried almost entirely beneath the couch pillows. "Where do they come up with this stuff? I mean, it's just so weird. . . ."

Matt pulled his head out of the sofa to take a look at what he had collected so far. Lanny did the same.

"Okay," Matt said, peering at the junk in his palm. He decided not to count the lint he had gathered. "A nickel, two pennies, a peppermint candy, and a bunch of nuts." He tossed the nuts over his shoulder, then pointed to a weird, leathery thing that looked like an ancient piece of jerky. "I don't know what that is." Matt picked up a black, fossilized shell-like object. "And I think this is the turtle I lost three years ago."

Lanny took the shriveled turtle from Matt, stared at it a minute, then stuffed it in his pocket.

"Well, c'mon," Matt said with a shrug. Seven cents and a peppermint candy wouldn't exactly get them the walkie-talkies of their dreams, so it was clearly time for a new plan. "We'd better go start checking pay phones for change."

Lizzie and Gordo settled into their auditorium seats to watch Miranda's rehearsal. Lizzie had a mini tape recorder and a small notebook with her so that she could take notes for the school Webzine. Gordo was just along for the ride . . . and to fascinate Lizzie with facts about who-knows-what, no doubt.

Oooh, Miranda is so lucky, Lizzie thought as she looked at the stage where Miranda stood next to superhot Travis Elliot who was playing the male lead.

"Okay. Places, everyone!" Mr. Escobar shouted. He was a slightly chunky man in his early forties, and he always wore a blue silk scarf around his neck, even in the summer.

"After rehearsal, I'm going to ask Mr. Escobar a few questions," Lizzie whispered to Gordo. "How the play got started, how he got the ideas for the show—"

"What's up with that blue scarf he always wears . . ." Gordo added, nodding.

Lizzie shushed him, afraid that Mr. Escobar might hear. But the drama teacher was way too busy getting lost in the moment onstage.

"'Listen, Rhonda,'" Travis read from his script. "'I got to get outta this town.'" Travis pounded his chest dramatically. "'My old man, he just doesn't understand.'"

"'Oh, Reb,'" Miranda said in a voice that sounded like she was reading the ingredients on the back of a shampoo bottle, "'be strong for both of us. *Rhonda walks to the table, worried.*'" Miranda walked over to the table . . . apparently, worried.

"Okay, hold on a second, Miranda," Mr. Escobar said quickly. "That was great, we're on our way to the stars!" he gushed. "But '*Rhonda walks to the table, worried*'—it isn't dialogue—you actually *do* it." Mr. Escobar flicked his blue scarf over his shoulder and walked over to Travis. "It's 'Oh, Reb, be strong for the both of us,'" he demonstrated, taking on the part of Rhonda as though he were born to play the role. "And you walk to the table, worried," he added, striding over to the table, a concerned expression on his face. "But you don't have to say it." He broke character and smiled brightly at Miranda.

"Oh, right, right!" Miranda nodded furiously. "Mr. Escobar, I just want to thank you again for letting me be in this play. Acting is, like, the greatest thing I've ever done."

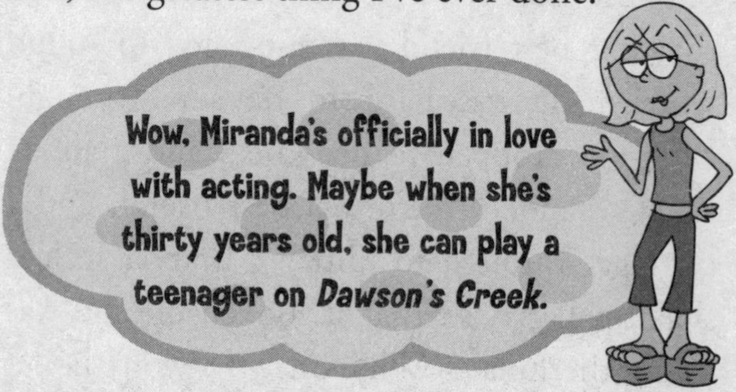

Wow, Miranda's officially in love with acting. Maybe when she's thirty years old, she can play a teenager on *Dawson's Creek*.

"You're very welcome, Miranda," Mr. Escobar said generously. "Let's move on to the drag race scene, shall we?" he shouted. "Larry, care to join us?"

Larry Tudgeman loped onstage.

"Heh-heh," Gordo chuckled. "It's Tudgeman."

Lizzie scowled at him. How could she pay attention to the play when he was busy distracting her?

"'Oh! Stingo!'" Miranda cried. "'Why does Reb do such dangerous things?'" Miranda was using her shampoo-bottle voice again, only this time it was louder, so Lizzie guessed that her best friend was supposed to sound worried. It was hard to be sure, though. Miranda dropped to her knees and grabbed Larry's hand. "'You're his best friend, and I can't get through to him.'" Miranda started shaking Larry, so that it looked like he was doing the hula. "'Why, oh why, won't he let me in?'"

Mr. Escobar watched the action, clearly mesmerized. He was mouthing the words along with Miranda.

Gordo leaned toward Lizzie. “How come this is so lame?” he whispered.

“It’s just rehearsal,” Lizzie said defensively. “I mean, I’m sure the movie with the hockey-playing chimp wasn’t brilliant the first time they ran through it. It’ll get better.”

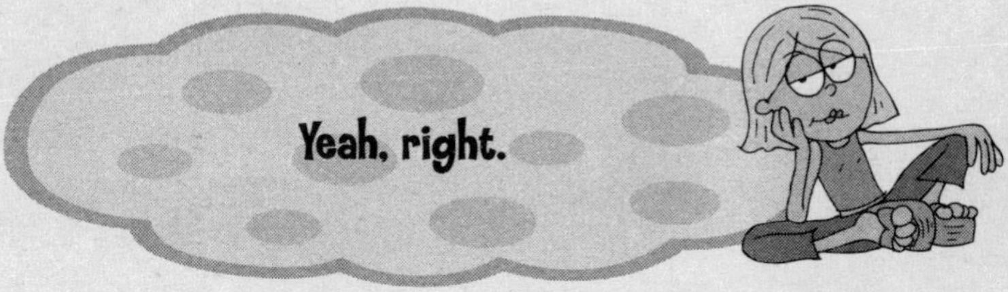

Onstage, Miranda had grabbed Larry’s shirt and was nearly strangling him. “‘Can’t you talk some sense into him, Tudgeman?’” she demanded.

Larry looked around, unsure how to respond. “Um . . . I’m Stingo, remember?” he murmured.

“Oh, ‘Can’t you talk some sense into him, *Stingo*?’” Miranda cried.

Lizzie swallowed hard. "At least I sure *hope* it gets better," she added. One thing was for sure . . . this play had a long way to go before it was halfway as good as that hockey-playing chimp movie.

CHAPTER THREE

Matt and Lanny plodded into Matt's bedroom and sat down on the couch. Matt carried a tray, which he put on his blue trunk at the end of his bed. On the tray were two large glasses of orange soda and a sugar bowl.

"I can't believe that garage sale your parents had," Matt said as he spooned some sugar from the bowl into each glass of orange soda. "I never knew people would pay money for old junk." He gestured to his neck. "I mean, that lady with that weird purple thing on her neck paid five dollars for a cookie jar shaped like an elf."

Lanny looked around Matt's room and then looked at Matt.

"Hey," Matt said slowly. "I think I'm thinking what you're thinking." He peered around his room. There was stuff everywhere—crammed onto bookshelves, overflowing the closet, threatening to escape the dresser. There it was—the answer to their walkie-talkie problem. The idea was so obvious; Matt couldn't believe that he and Lanny hadn't thought of it before! "Sell *my* stuff! I've got a *roomful* of junk I could get rid of. Then we'll have the money for the walkie-talkies."

Lanny nodded and grinned, barely able to contain his excitement.

Matt raised his glass in a toast. "Here's to money," Matt said.

He and Lanny tossed back the extra sweetened orange soda. Lanny made a face.

"Oh, sorry, Lanny," Matt said quickly. "My bad. Here—" he picked up the sugar bowl and dumped the whole thing into Lanny's glass. Lanny grinned and took a huge gulp.

Now everything was just perfect.

Lizzie looked around, trying to find Miranda. It was opening night of the play, and Lizzie was backstage, where everyone was bustling around, making last-minute adjustments to their wardrobes, practicing lines, and checking their hair and makeup.

Lizzie spotted Miranda nearby. She looked great! She was wearing a white sweater and a blue poodle skirt.

"Miranda!" Lizzie called.

"Hey!" Miranda said, smiling warmly. She glanced over her shoulder to where Mr.

Escobar was rounding up the rest of the cast. "Oh, I don't have much time—Mr. Escobar makes us meditate before we go on," she explained.

"That outfit is *so* excellent," Lizzie said, grinning at Miranda's poodle skirt.

"Thanks." Miranda smiled and clapped in excitement. "I'm going to be a star!"

"And I'm going to write about it!" Lizzie added, waving her mini tape recorder. Lizzie held out a small stuffed cow. "Here—" she said to Miranda.

Miranda looked confused. "It's Cindy Lou Moo," she said.

Lizzie nodded. "Yeah. You gave her to me before soccer play-offs, and it helped me score a goal. So now she's going to bring *you* some good luck." *I hope*, Lizzie added mentally.

"Thanks," Miranda said as she wrapped Lizzie in a warm hug.

"Gather 'round, kids," Mr. Escobar called.

"Thanks," Miranda said again, holding up Cindy Lou Moo and smiling. "I got to go."

"Okay." Lizzie bit her lip as Miranda scampered off to join the rest of the cast. They were already deep in meditation, chanting "*Ommmm.*"

Lizzie sighed. She hoped that the chanting would help. She hadn't seen the play since the disastrous rehearsal and just hoped that it had got at least a little bit better. Please, just let this play be as good as the movie about the hockey-playing chimp, Lizzie begged silently. Oh, who am I kidding? She added as she made her way toward the audience, where Gordo was saving her a seat. Like anything could be that good!

Lizzie slid into the seat next to Gordo, who had brought his video camera. The school play was a fund-raiser, so Lizzie had talked her parents into coming, and into bringing Matt and Lanny, too. Unsurprisingly, Matt wasn't even paying attention. He was just sitting next to Lanny, playing a video game. Lanny was asleep.

"Is Miranda nervous?" Gordo asked Lizzie.

"No," Lizzie said. "I've never seen her so confident." That must be a good sign, Lizzie said to herself. It *has* to be a good sign, right?

Just then, the lights went down. Lizzie sat back in her chair and held on to the armrests. Showtime.

"Here we go . . ." Mrs. McGuire said eagerly.

"Yup, here we go . . ." Mr. McGuire agreed, not quite so eagerly. He checked his watch.

Lizzie tried to ignore him. After all, he *was* here for Miranda's big debut. And he *had* paid for the tickets. And that was all that mattered.

The curtain went up, revealing the interior of a fifties-style malt shop. Travis walked onstage in jeans and a leather jacket right out of a 1950s movie. Larry spotted him and walked over. He was wearing suspenders and a bow tie, and—although it hardly seemed possible—looked like an even bigger dork than usual.

"'Hey, Reb!'" Larry said to Travis. "'I heard you got expelled from school.'"

"Heh-heh," said the kid sitting in front of Lizzie. "It's Tudgeman."

Lizzie glared at the back of the kid's head.

"'That's right, Stingo,'" Travis said. "'That lousy vice principal Mr. Birch hasn't liked me since my family's moved west and I started here at South East Northfield High.'"

"'Man, that's a gyp, Reb,'" Larry said, shaking his head. "'They should've launched *him* into orbit, instead of the astronauts! Oh!'" Larry poked his finger in the air and made a goofy face.

The audience was silent.

"'Ah, Stingo—'" Travis said, grinning broadly, "'you and your wisecracks!'"

"'Reb! Reb!'" Miranda shouted as she ran onstage. She trotted into the scene and slammed her leg into a jukebox. "Oh!" she cried, clearly startled. But she just plowed ahead, limping over to Travis and Larry. "'Now that you've been expelled, my father will never let me see you again. I'll be resticted. *Stricted.* I'll be re*strict*ed.'" Miranda rolled her eyes and grimaced. "My bad," she said through clenched teeth. She shook her head and went on. "'And the senior prom is two weeks away!'" Miranda gestured dramatically and knocked a glass off a nearby table.

Lizzie looked over at Gordo. This was not going well. And Lizzie had the feeling that it was about to get worse.

Bring on the chimp, Lizzie thought miserably.

* * *

"'Reb? REB!'" Miranda screeched onstage. She whirled toward Andy Matthews, the kid playing her father. "'How could you do that, Daddy?'" she wailed, sirenlike. "'You'll never understand Reb because he's a wild Mustang running free as swiftly as the eagle on the prairie flying above us—'" Miranda caught her breath and went on. "'The wide-open spaces—'" She flailed her arms, knocking over a vase of flowers.

Lizzie winced. With every passing moment, this play just got worse in ways that were difficult to believe, much less predict.

"'So, I'm going with Reb, even if I have to drop out of school. I guess now I'll never be—'" Miranda punched the air dramatically. "'Be— be—'" She groped for the word, then pulled back her sleeve and peered at her wrist. "'Valedictorian,'" Miranda finished. She yanked her sleeve back into place, and then turned toward the door. "'Wait for me, Reb!'" she shouted, scurrying offstage. Unfortunately, she ran into a ladder that was propped up behind the set. The ladder fell over onto the side of the set, and the whole thing creaked and groaned, then came crashing down. Miranda stopped in her tracks, stared at the set, then turned and went ahead, hurrying offstage.

Lizzie looked at Gordo.

"It didn't get any better," Gordo said.

Lizzie just couldn't deny the truth anymore. "It's official," she agreed. "Miranda stinks."

Matt put the last plastic toy into a box. He and Lanny had been packing and stacking for hours, but it finally looked as though their garage sale was coming together. They were placing all of the boxes in Matt's red Radio Flyer wagon, so they could haul it over to the school parking lot, where they planned to make their walkie-talkie fortune.

"Be careful with that box, Lanny," Matt commanded as Lanny picked up another box for the pile. "I've got a Celine Dion snow globe in there." He rolled his eyes. "That's got to be worth at least five bucks to *some* yokel."

Lanny gently placed the box with the snow globe on top of the others. Then he reached for another box and put it next to the last one.

"No, Lanny, I told you—" Matt said, "first, we're selling the books, then the toys, then the clothes. And then we'll sell the wagon."

Lanny removed the box.

"Okay, are you ready, Lanny?"

Lanny rubbed his hands together and nodded eagerly.

"Hey, Matt. Lanny." Gordo said as he

walked out onto the deck. "Uh, is your sister here?" Gordo asked Matt.

Matt jerked his head toward the door. "She's inside," he said. "Hey, we're selling some of my old stuff—wanna buy anything?" He pulled out a water gun and handed it to Gordo, smiling enticingly.

Gordo lifted his eyebrows as he stared at Matt's boxed-up junk. "I don't think so."

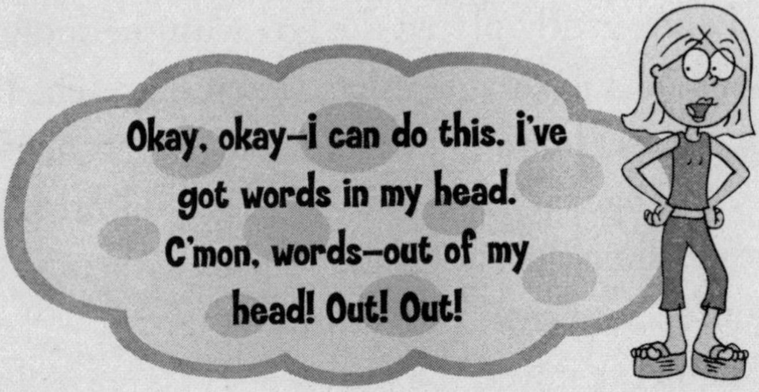

Okay, okay—i can do this. i've got words in my head. C'mon, words—out of my head! Out! Out!

Lizzie was sitting on the couch in the living room, trying to write up her review of Miranda's play. But nothing was coming to her. That is, nothing that would allow her to remain friends with Miranda was coming to her. Her mind was a blank slate, other than the words, "Horrible beyond belief."

Let's go, Lizzie told herself. Work with me, brain! Give me something!

Suddenly, something popped into her head, and she scribbled it down. Lizzie stared at what she had written in her notebook.

Scranton, it said.

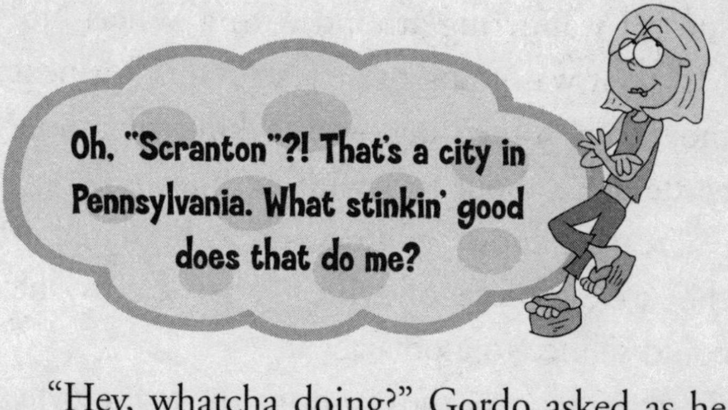

Oh, "Scranton"?! That's a city in Pennsylvania. What stinkin' good does that do me?

"Hey, whatcha doing?" Gordo asked as he loped into the living room. He was carrying something that looked like a bent wire hanger.

"The play review," Lizzie said miserably.

She stared at the wire thingy in Gordo's hand. "What's that?"

Gordo flopped onto the couch next to Lizzie and sighed. "A Wheel-O."

"It doesn't have a wheel," Lizzie pointed out. I thought that the whole point of a Wheel-O is to have the wheel magically go up and around the wire, Lizzie mused. But she guessed that Gordo must have some good reason for wandering around with a Wheel-No. Maybe it was going to be featured in his next movie, or something—some kind of avant-garde piece about toys with no purpose.

"Yeah, I know," Gordo said as he stared at the useless piece of wire. "That Lanny, he could sell ice to a polar bear."

Okay, scratch the avant-garde toy movie, Lizzie thought. I should have known that this broken toy thing had something to do with my annoying little brother and his weirdo friend.

She wondered how Silent Lanny had sold Gordo the broken Wheel-O. Could he turn his eyes into hypnosis wheels, or something?

"So, how's the review coming?" Gordo asked.

"Mmm, great!" Lizzie said sarcastically. "Just great!" She handed her notebook to Gordo.

"'*Greasier* Review,'" Gordo read. "'By Lizzie McGuire . . . Scranton.'" Gordo stared at the page for a moment, as though waiting for more words to appear. When they didn't, he finally said, "Well, that really says it all. I probably would've gone with 'Pittsburgh,' but you know me, I overstate things."

Lizzie grabbed the notebook back. "That's just doodling," she said defensively. "I can't bring myself to say that Miranda. . . ."

Gordo lifted his eyebrows. "Stinks like a cab driver's armpit?" he guessed.

"Gordo!" Lizzie cried. "I can't say that. She's my best friend—I can't give her a bad review."

"It's not a big deal," Gordo said calmly. "Miranda's an actress—she knows that sometimes you don't get good reviews."

Lizzie rolled her eyes. Sure, that was easy for Gordo to say. He wasn't the one who had to *write* the lousy review. All he had to do was sit around and think of words like "Pittsburgh." "But she's counting on me to support her," Lizzie protested.

"She may be the worst actress in history," Gordo said reasonably, "and you're reporting on it—you have to report the truth."

Lizzie bit her lip and looked down at her paper. "Well, I may have to report the truth, but that doesn't mean I can't go easy on her." She sighed and started writing. "Newcomer Miranda Sanchez gives her best effort as Rhonda, in the school production of *Greasier*," she scribbled.

I just hope that Gordo is right, Lizzie

thought as she scrawled across the page. Otherwise, I'm completely dead.

"'Unfortunately, her best effort comes up short,'" Miranda read aloud from the page she had printed out from the school Webzine. She looked up at Lizzie, and gave her a look that Lizzie knew well—it was Miranda's version of pure rage, and it was a pretty scary thing.

Yup. I guess I *am* completely dead, after all, Lizzie thought.

"Comes up short?" Miranda demanded, brandishing the Webzine article like a paper weapon.

Please don't give me a paper cut, Lizzie thought as she eyed the article in Miranda's hand. "Well, I said your clothes looked nice," Lizzie pointed out quickly.

"How could you do this?" Miranda growled.

"You know how important this play is to me!"

"I know—" Lizzie said apologetically. *Where is Gordo when I need him?* she thought frantically. *Why can't he be here to tell Miranda about reporting the truth and accepting bad reviews gracefully and all that other junk he said yesterday?* "And I—"

"I can't believe it," Miranda said. There was a catch in her voice, and Lizzie could tell that her friend was really hurt. "I thought you were my best friend!"

Miranda turned and ran down the steps before Lizzie could say anything else.

I never knew that journalism could be so dangerous, Lizzie thought miserably. *Maybe Mr. Lang has the right idea—I should just get myself a book of crossword puzzles and hide in my room . . . for the rest of my life.*

CHAPTER FOUR

Lizzie looked around the lunchroom and finally spotted Miranda sitting at a table in the corner, eating alone. Lizzie looked over at Gordo, who nodded. She took a deep breath. It was now or never. After all, Miranda had to get over being mad sometime, right?

Oh, please, get over being mad, Lizzie thought as she walked toward Miranda. I hate it when you're mad.

"Hey, Miranda," Lizzie said softly as she

pulled a chair up next to Miranda's. "I got you some flan," she said, holding out a dish of the Mexican custard. "I know how much you like it." Lizzie put the dish in front of her friend. Miranda looked down at the flan like it was a plate of slug fondue and slid down to the end of the table.

Hey! Don't slide away from me, Miss Thing! I'm trying to be the nice one here!

Lizzie scooted her chair closer to Miranda, who scooched away. Okay, don't get mad, Lizzie told herself. Miranda's feelings are hurt—she'll come around. "Come on, Miranda," Lizzie pleaded. "I mean—I didn't mean for the review to hurt you."

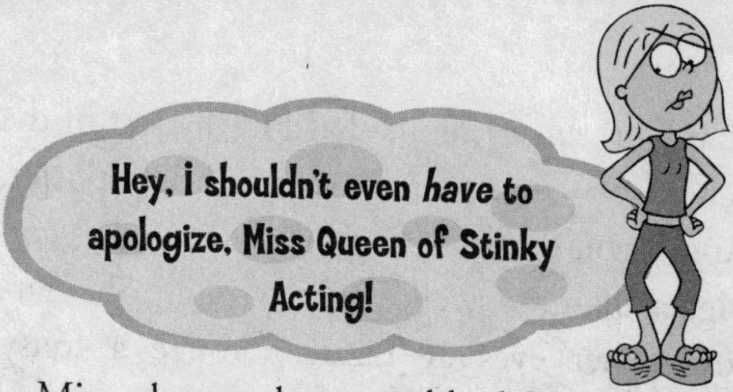

Hey, i shouldn't even *have* to apologize, Miss Queen of Stinky Acting!

Miranda stood up, grabbed her tray, and walked over to the trash can. She slammed her tray on top of the can like it was the can's fault that Lizzie had written the review.

Okay, now this was getting annoying. After all, Lizzie thought, I only wrote the truth. I thought that the truth was supposed to set you free—not make people hate you. Lizzie took a deep breath. Just try to stay calm, Lizzie thought. There's no point in getting angry.

"I was just trying to do my job," Lizzie explained. "I thought that you would understand."

"Oh, I understand," Miranda said. Her voice was trembling with anger. "I understand that you're just jealous that I'm the star of the school play and you are just a little reporter. And if you think tearing me down makes you bigger than me, well, you're wrong." She narrowed her eyes at Lizzie. "You're a lousy friend." She turned to stamp away.

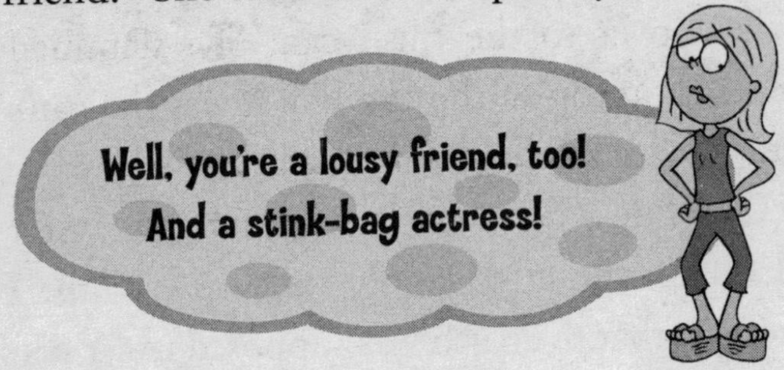
Well, you're a lousy friend, too!
And a stink-bag actress!

"Well, you're a lousy friend, too!" Lizzie shouted. "And a stink-bag actress!"

Whoa, Lizzie thought. Did I just say that out loud?

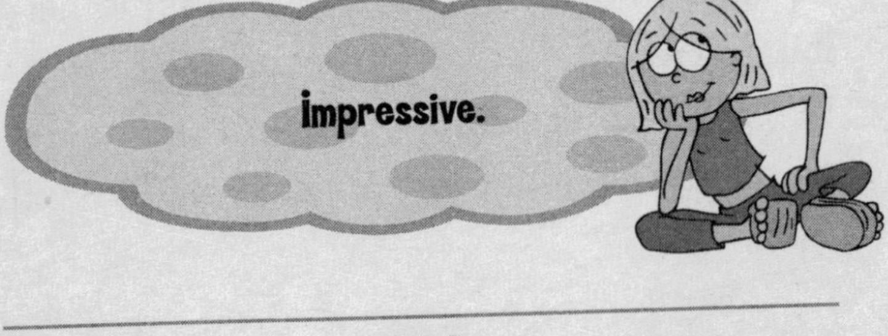
impressive.

Wasn't I supposed to be controlling my anger? Lizzie thought. Still, she had to admit—getting mad felt kind of good.

Lizzie turned to storm off, and saw Gordo sitting at the end of the table, eating the flan Lizzie had bought for Miranda. Lizzie didn't have time to yell at Gordo, though, because just then, Larry Tudgeman walked by with a plate full of fries. Miranda grabbed the fries and chucked them at Lizzie before finally storming off. Luckily, most of them missed. And even more luckily it was fries she had flung, and not that Broccoli Surprise!

Gordo cocked an eyebrow at Lizzie. "Didn't go so well, huh?"

"Aw, those are my fries!" Larry wailed.

Lizzie scowled at Gordo, who took another bite of the flan. "Brilliant observation, Gordo," Lizzie said sarcastically.

This whole situation was getting out of control.

"Miranda, wait up," Gordo called.

Miranda wheeled around to face him. "Don't even try to defend Lizzie, Gordo," she said, folding her arms across her chest.

Gordo held something out to Miranda. "I don't have to," Gordo said.

Miranda frowned confusedly at the things in Gordo's hands.

"This is a tape of your performance," Gordo explained. "And this is the review Lizzie wrote. Take a good look at them both." He handed them to Miranda—then he walked away.

Miranda looked down at the tape in her hand. She hesitated a moment, then shrugged off her fear. She knew that she didn't have anything to worry about—her acting was great. After all, how could she be lousy at something that she loved so much? It wasn't possible.

Miranda squared her shoulders and walked toward the Webzine office. There was a VCR in there. Miranda figured that she could watch the tape, and then leave it in the office as proof that Lizzie's review had been unfair.

Luckily, the Webzine office was deserted when Miranda got there. She popped the tape into the VCR, then sat back to watch her performance. Her stomach tightened a little as the tape began to play, but she forced herself to relax. Miranda knew that she couldn't possibly be half as bad as Lizzie's review said that she was. In fact, she was even kind of eager to see herself onstage—as a star!

Then the tape started playing.

"'Oh, Reb, I've found you at last.'"

Miranda watched herself walk across the

stage like she was made of wood. She had to admit, her acting voice sounded a little like the voice her mom used when reading off a shopping list.

"'Don't move—'" Miranda watched herself say on the screen. "'I'm coming across this arcade and—'"

A loud crash erupted from the TV screen. The tape had reached the part when Miranda had accidentally knocked over a bucket of dishes that the kid playing the busboy was carrying as a prop. "Oops—ow—" Miranda watched herself stumble into a trash can.

Miranda slid down in her chair. The tape didn't stop, and it just kept getting worse and worse. . . .

"'—And jumping into your arms and never letting go!'" Onscreen, Miranda knocked over a parrot cage. Mr. Escobar's bird, which he had loaned to the production for the pivotal pet store scene, let out a loud squawk. "Sorry . . ." Miranda watched herself apologize to the parrot.

Miranda sighed and shook her head. She had to admit it—she stank worse than one of Gordo's sweat socks.

The only question was . . . what was she going to do about it?

"Roger that, Lanny," Matt said into his shiny new walkie-talkie as he ran through the hallway. "I'm exiting the kitchen, and heading upstairs. Will establish communications from there. Matt over and out."

Mrs. McGuire and her husband stared at one another. When they had told Matt to go out and earn his own money for the walkie-talkies, neither one of them had expected him to actually go out and *do* it. So, how had this happened?

"Honey?" Mrs. McGuire called up to Matt from the bottom of the stairs.

Matt stopped and smiled at her.

"Honey? Where'd you get the walkie-talkies?" Mrs. McGuire asked.

"I earned them, like you said," Matt explained proudly. "Well, I got to go. Lanny got his stomach pumped, and he's going to tell me all about it." Matt ran to the top of the stairs.

Mrs. McGuire gave her husband a worried frown.

"How did he earn all that money?" Mr. McGuire asked.

"And what did Lanny eat?" Mrs. McGuire added.

Clearly, this was a situation that deserved further investigation, so Mr. and Mrs. McGuire headed upstairs to talk to Matt.

"So, even though they *look* like marshmallows, they don't really *taste* like marshmallows,"

Matt was saying into his walkie-talkie. "That's good to know. Well, Matt, over and out. Talk to you later."

Mr. and Mrs. McGuire walked into Matt's room. The first thing Mrs. McGuire noticed was that Matt's room was cleaner than it had been in years. She felt a brief moment of pleasure before she realized that Matt's room was clean because it was completely empty.

There were no toys. No books. No clothes. Matt even seemed to have sold the dust bunnies in the corner. All he had left were his four favorite things—Mr. Rooster, the stuffed animal; a plastic monkey that Mr. McGuire had given him when Matt went away to sleepaway camp; a bowling pin; and a plastic golden crown.

Matt was lying on a beach towel in the middle of the floor. Even his bed had disappeared.

"Hey, Matt," Mr. McGuire said slowly. He didn't really know what to say after that, so he just stopped and stared at the empty room, completely dumbfounded.

"What happened to all your things, honey?" Mrs. McGuire asked.

Matt shrugged. "Sold 'em," he said casually.

"And you used the money for your walkie-talkie?" Mr. McGuire asked. His voice was kind of strangled.

"Uh, yeah!" Matt grinned and held up the walkie-talkie. He hauled himself to his feet and dusted himself off. "Well, I got to go downstairs and do my spelling homework." Matt turned to walk away, and then seemed to remember something. "Oh, yeah. I don't have anything to wear tomorrow to school. See ya!" Matt scurried out of the room.

Mrs. McGuire stared around the room.

“What’s it going to cost to replace all his stuff?” she asked.

“Uh . . .” Mr. McGuire seemed incapable of speech.

Mrs. McGuire nodded. “Right.”

“Yeah.” Mr. McGuire cleared his throat.

“Let’s not teach him anything else for a while, okay?” Mrs. McGuire said.

“Okay,” Mr. McGuire agreed.

After all, they couldn’t really afford to.

CHAPTER FIVE

Mrs. McGuire stood at the kitchen counter, packing a sandwich and some fruit into a picnic basket.

"Hey, Mom," Lizzie said as she walked into the kitchen. "I think I'm going to buy my lunch at school tomorrow, so you don't need to pack me one."

"Honey, this isn't for you," Mrs. McGuire explained. "This is for your dad's softball game."

Lizzie scoffed. "You're going to Dad's softball game?"

Her mom chuckled and nodded. “Mm, hmm.”

“But he hardly even gets to play,” Lizzie protested. “And the only time he gets to a base is when he gets hit by a pitch.” This was true. Lizzie had been to a game once, and her father had struck out every single time until he finally got whacked on the batting helmet by a wild pitch.

Mrs. McGuire shrugged. “Well, his team finally made it to the semi-quarter consolation game, whatever. And it’s the best they’ve ever done, so I figured, what the heck.”

Lizzie frowned. This still wasn’t making sense. “But you don’t even like softball.”

“Honey, it’s not that I ‘don’t like’ it,” Mrs. McGuire said patiently. “I hate it. It’s very, very dull to watch, and the bleachers are incredibly uncomfortable.”

Lizzie knew that was only half of it. Her mom always ended up sitting with some of

Dad's friends, who had chili dog breath and shouted at the umpire at every play.

"Well, *he* didn't go to your blood drive," Lizzie pointed out.

"Well, to be fair, he was working that day," Mrs. McGuire said loyally.

Lizzie scoffed. "I thought he just didn't want to go."

"Well, if he did, I would still go to his game," Mrs. McGuire replied. "It's not about who owes who what—if you love someone, you support them."

Lizzie swallowed hard. She didn't like the way this conversation was going.

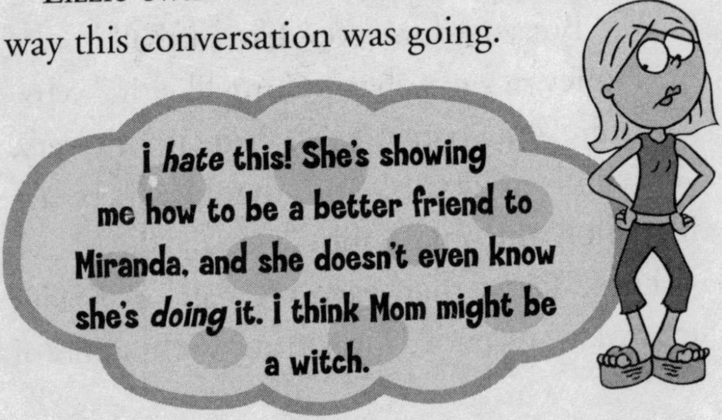

i *hate* this! She's showing me how to be a better friend to Miranda. and she doesn't even know she's *doing* it. i think Mom might be a witch.

Lizzie watched her mom put a bottle of aspirin into the picnic basket. Look at that, Lizzie thought. Mom is going to the game *and* she's realistic about it.

Lizzie still didn't really know why her mom was going to this silly softball game, but she did know one thing . . . she had to talk to Miranda, as soon as possible. And that meant going back to the school play . . . right now.

When Lizzie arrived backstage, Mr. Escobar was reading Lizzie's review to the cast.

"In spite of the efforts of the rest of the cast, the entire play is dragged down by Miranda Sanchez's performance," he read. Mr. Escobar, clearly upset, had to press his lips together to keep from crying. He looked up from the review and spotted Lizzie. "You . . ." he said angrily. "I . . ." He looked at the ceiling and shook his head sadly. "We were on our way to the stars," he wailed. Then he took a deep breath and collected himself. "Places, everyone," he called.

The cast shuffled to their places. All except Miranda, who turned to face Lizzie. Lizzie noticed that her friend was holding Cindy Lou Moo, and decided to take it as a good sign.

"Miranda," Lizzie said in a rush. She knew that she had to be quick—the play was already starting. "I know you think I'm a terrible friend, but before you drop a spotlight on me, I wanted to show you this—" She handed Miranda a piece of paper.

Miranda scanned the paper. It was another review.

"It's running in the next issue," Lizzie explained. "It's a retraction of my review."

"'Contrary to previous reports, Miranda

Sanchez is very entertaining as Rhonda Doppoppolis,'" Miranda read aloud. She looked up at Lizzie dubiously.

"I was wrong to run a bad review," Lizzie said sincerely. "And I'm really sorry."

"No," Miranda said slowly as she handed the retraction back to Lizzie, "you're wrong *now.* I was terrible."

"You were terrible?" Lizzie repeated.

"I saw the tape of my performance. Phew! I even wrote a letter to the editor, saying your review was too nice. How can you write a retraction of the truth?"

Lizzie swallowed hard. "Because you're my friend and you love acting. I couldn't just ruin that for you."

Miranda smiled weakly. "Well . . . thanks. But just because I'm a bad actress doesn't mean you should be a bad journalist."

"Well, if I'd known it was going to make

you feel *that* bad, I would've never written the review," Lizzie said.

"Thanks," Miranda said, "but if I'd known I was going to stink that bad, I would've never even done the show. I'm sorry I got mad at you. But, let's face it, acting is not my thing."

Miranda handed Cindy Lou Moo to Lizzie.

From somewhere far away, Lizzie heard someone say, "'Oh, Stingo—you and your wisecracks.'" She knew there was something important about that line, but she couldn't remember what it was.

Miranda smiled at Lizzie, and Lizzie smiled back.

"Hey, maybe Glee Club!" Miranda said suddenly.

"Huh?" Lizzie asked. All at once, she felt as though she had missed an important part of the conversation.

"'OH, STINGO—YOU AND YOUR

WISECRACKS!'" the voice repeated onstage.

Why does Travis keep saying that? Lizzie thought, annoyed.

"Glee Club," Miranda explained. "If I'm a bad actress, I have to be a good singer."

Lizzie nodded uncertainly. There was a definite logic to that thought—certainly Madonna was proof of it. Then again, what if Miranda was even worse at singing than acting? All I know is that there's no way I'm writing a review for Glee Club, Lizzie thought.

Glee Club . . . ? Singing . . . ?
Oh, no.

"'OH, STINGO—YOU AND YOUR WISECRACKS!'" Travis shouted.

Miranda looked over toward the stage. "Oops, that's my cue," she said. Then she shook her head and smiled at Lizzie. "Poor audience," she murmured, and hurried onstage, calling, "'Reb! Reb!'" Miranda ran into a table. "Ow!"

Singing. Just when you think Miranda's hit bottom, she gets a shovel.

A month later, Lizzie and Gordo found themselves back in the school auditorium. It was Glee Club recital, and Lizzie was so nervous, she was afraid that she might actually barf. Just tell her that you've never heard singing like that before, Lizzie reminded herself, and then worked on rehearsing the line she'd spent an entire week coming up with in case Miranda's singing was utterly atrocious.

The spotlight came up, and Miranda was standing in the middle of the stage, alone. The music started.

Lizzie winced. I've never heard singing like that before, she practiced mentally. I've never heard singing like that before, I've never heard singing . . .

Then Miranda sang.

. . . like *that* before. . . . Suddenly, Lizzie realized something. Miranda was good. As in, really good.

How could I have been friends with Miranda for all this time and never known that she was such a talented singer? Lizzie wondered, amazed that there could still be things about her best friend that she didn't know.

Gordo looked over at Lizzie and smiled. She was glad that he was taping *this* performance. Lizzie knew that they wouldn't have to have a videocassette-burning ceremony this time, the way they had done with the video of *Greasier*.

"Hello, Mariah Carey!" Lizzie whispered to Gordo.

"She really found something she doesn't stink at," Gordo added.

Good for Miranda. i bet if i keep looking, i'll find the thing i'm really good at, too.

Miranda continued to sing. It was like the music was coming straight from her soul. You go, Miranda!

Lizzie looked over at Gordo, who was watching the recital through the lens of his video camera, and smiled. I always knew that my friends were amazing, Lizzie thought as she sat back to enjoy the show, and now I'll have the videotape to prove it.

Don't close the book on Lizzie yet! Here's a sneak peek at the next Lizzie McGuire story. . . .

Best Dressed

Adapted by Jasmine Jones
Based on the series created by Terri Minsky
Based on a teleplay written by Bob Thomas

"I saw the grossest thing this morning," Lizzie McGuire said as she walked toward homeroom with her best friends, David "Gordo" Gordon and Miranda Sanchez. "And it was floating," Lizzie added. She shuddered at the memory. The truth was, she wasn't one hundred percent sure what the thing was, although she had a few ideas—all repulsive. Lizzie definitely knew something gross when she saw it. She did, after all, have a little brother, and Matt McGuire was pretty much the master of revolting stuff.

"In the air?" Gordo asked, seemingly intrigued by the unnamed floating grossness.

Miranda curled her lip at him and blinked. Gordo was a good friend, but he could be kind of peculiar.

"No, no," Lizzie said. She jerked her head toward the exit doors. "In the water fountain outside the school," she explained. The three friends walked into class and plopped into their chairs.

Miranda grimaced. "I don't want to hear about this."

"I do," Gordo said eagerly.

Miranda groaned as a shriek of feedback blasted out from the loudspeakers. Lizzie plugged her ears. The annoying (not to mention painful!) sound lasted a few moments before the voice of the equally annoying, nerdiest kid in the universe—Larry Tudgeman—came over the loudspeaker.

"Good morning," Larry said brightly. "Lawrence Tudgeman the third here with your morning announcements."

"So, what exactly was floating in the water fountain?" Gordo whispered as he leaned toward Lizzie.

Lizzie made a sour face. How could she possibly describe the gross thing she had seen? It was beyond description.

"So, whoever put the . . . *you-know-what* in the water fountain this morning," Larry droned over the PA system, "the principal's going to find out who you are . . . *Joey.*"

Lizzie rolled her eyes. Was Larry Tudgeman insane? Joey Wannamaker is the biggest bully in the school, she thought. And she meant "biggest" literally. The rumor was that Joey had actually flunked seventh grade eight times. And he certainly looked more like a college sophomore than a junior high school student. Not that he looked as smart or mature or anything—he was just . . . big!

"I mean, not that I would tell anybody, *Joey* . . ." Larry's voice droned on over the loudspeaker, "so let's just forget that I ever said it, okay, *Joey* . . ."

Lizzie rolled her eyes. She could just picture Larry wearing that know-it-all smile of his as he sat behind the microphone.

"I would not want to be Joey," Miranda said.

Gordo lifted an eyebrow. "I would not want to be *Tudgeman.*"

Good point, Lizzie thought.

"Anyway . . ." Larry went on, switching into his official "news announcement" voice, "next Monday we will be voting on class favorites."

Gordo snorted. "Great. Yet another opportunity to make students feel inadequate." He shook his head.

Larry's voice droned on. "The categories are Best Looking—"

Lizzie looked at the ceiling and sighed. "Cheerleader," she said. Miranda flashed her a look that said "of course."

"—Best Dressed—" Larry said.

Miranda twirled her hair and rolled her eyes. "Cheerleader," she said in a mock-perky voice.

"Most Poised," Larry went on, "and Most Likely to Succeed. Hi, Joey."

Suddenly, there was another shriek of feedback. Then, several loud *thunks* barked from the loudspeaker.

Gordo sat back in his chair and shuddered at the noise. "I guess the announcements are over," he said.

Something is definitely over, Lizzie thought. She just hoped that it wasn't Larry's life.

Just then, the bell rang. Lizzie hauled herself out of her seat toward her first-period class.

"So, who do you think will win Best Looking?" Miranda asked as she slung her book bag over her shoulder.

Lizzie shrugged. There were really only two possibilities. "Kate or Claire," Lizzie said, naming the two snobbiest and most popular girls in the school. They were the ultimate queen bees . . . and both were cheerleaders, of course.

Miranda nodded. "What about Best Dressed?"

Lizzie scoffed, again thinking about the only two possible candidates. "Whoever doesn't win Best Looking."

Miranda pressed her lips together. "How about Most Poised?" she asked.

"Hey!" Lizzie said brightly, seeing a chink in the cheerleader armor. "I could win that one."

Gordo cocked an eyebrow. "Poised?" he said, pointing dubiously toward Lizzie. "Balanced? Easy manner? Graceful?"

Lizzie frowned at Gordo. Okay, it was true—there had been one or two times when she had opened her locker into her own face. And she guessed that she *had* tripped over her share of library carts that had been left carelessly in the middle of the hallway. Not to mention that incident with the green paint.

But that didn't mean that she wasn't poised, did it?

"Okay," Lizzie finally admitted briefly after thinking it over. "Maybe not." Still, she thought, that prize has to go to someone besides Kate or Claire. Someone with style. Someone who didn't fall down a lot. Someone like . . . Lizzie thought hard. "That sounds more like *you*, Miranda."

Miranda's eyebrows disappeared beneath the straight black line of her bangs. "You think?" She seemed really surprised by the idea.

"Yeah," Lizzie said quickly. "I mean, you haven't tripped, fallen, or spilled anything on yourself the whole entire year."

"Neither have I," Gordo pointed out.

Lizzie looked at him with half-closed eyes. Had Gordo completely forgotten the time he'd built the giant brain for science class that overloaded and exploded all over . . . well, all over *everything*? "Or blown up any science experiments," she added.

"That was a long time ago," Gordo said.

"People remember," Lizzie insisted. Believe me, she thought, an exploding brain is a difficult thing to forget. I've tried.

"Fine," Gordo huffed. "Then I'm going for Most Photographed This Year."

Lizzie frowned. "Is that even a category?"

"When the yearbook first comes out, what's the thing that everyone does?" Gordo demanded.

"Draw a mustache on Coach Kelly's picture?" Miranda suggested. Coach Kelly was the torturous gym teacher who actually considered square dancing a sport. She deserved that mustache.

Gordo shook his head. "No, no," he insisted.

"After that, they all count how many times they got their picture in it."

Lizzie thought about this for a moment. It was true. In fact, she usually went through the yearbook with a magnifying glass, just to make sure she hadn't missed any pictures of herself.

There's my hand! That counts!

Geez, how embarrassing. "I don't do that," Lizzie fibbed.

Gordo looked at her doubtfully. "How many times were you in the last yearbook?" he asked dryly.

"Three," Lizzie said automatically. Doh! Now she had given herself away. "I think it was three," she added slowly, as though she couldn't quite remember. She fiddled with her hair.

Gordo looked over at Miranda, who was doing the very same hair-fiddling thing as Lizzie, pretending she had no idea how many times her picture was in the yearbook. Gordo lifted his eyebrows in suspicious disbelief.

Miranda sighed. "Five," she admitted finally.

Lizzie smiled. Busted. Gordo was right, as usual.

"See?" Gordo asked. "Everybody keeps 'The Count.' So this year, I'm going to set a record. I'm going to be . . . *everywhere.*" He shook his head and added in his best Elvis Presley voice, "Thank you very much."

Lizzie laughed. Leave it to Gordo to come up with his own class-favorite category. And she had no doubt that he'd win it, too.

"Well, I definitely think that you are Most

Poised material," Lizzie said to Miranda later that day. Lizzie was shuffling through her locker, looking for her history notebook.

Miranda shrugged. "I don't really feel like 'Most' anything," she admitted.

"That's what Kate wants you to think," Gordo said, waving his hand dismissively. "That way you never even try. It's her way of maintaining the status quo."

Lizzie screwed up her face and frowned at Gordo. Couldn't he just speak English, like a normal person? "Status quo?" Lizzie repeated.

"It means that Kate wants to keep things the way they are," Gordo explained.

Miranda scowled at him. "Why didn't you just say that?" she snapped. Miranda had even less patience with Gordo's vocabulary than Lizzie did.

"Uh, I did," Gordo replied.

"Well, I say no more quo," Lizzie said

quickly. "If someone completely normal came to school on voting day dressed in an outrageously hip outfit, well, then they'd get the vote."

Gordo looked at her and nodded. "So—" he said, "—do it."

Lizzie blinked at him in surprise. "Me?" Why did Gordo have to pick today to take one of my suggestions seriously? she wondered.

"All you have to do is be better dressed than Kate or Claire for this one day," Gordo went on, like it would be the easiest thing in the world to outdress the coolest, hippest, most fabulous fashionistas to ever walk into their school.

But even Miranda was going along with the impossible dream. "And win Best Dressed," she added, smiling at Lizzie eagerly. "You can break the status cow!"

"Quo," Gordo corrected.

Miranda sighed impatiently. "Whatever," she snapped.

"I wouldn't know what to wear," Lizzie said uncertainly. She glanced down at her outfit—pink velour pants, belt with sparkly buckle, and pink-and-white tee: cute, but definitely not something that would set the fashion world on fire.

"There's a hot new pair of hip-huggers in the window at the Style Shack!" Miranda gushed. "All the music video people get clothes there. Kate and Claire might as well not even show up." Miranda smiled smugly.

"All you have to do is outdress Kate and Claire for one day," Gordo repeated, "and you'll be Best Dressed in the yearbook . . . forever."

Lizzie bit her lip. "Forever?"

Miranda lifted her eyebrows and nodded.

"Forever," Gordo replied.

Lizzie thought about that. Best Dressed . . . forever.

She just had to find a way to make this work!

Sorry! That's the end of the sneak peek for now. But don't go nuclear! To read the rest, all you have to do is look for the next title in the Lizzie McGuire series—

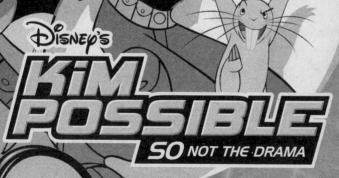

Lizzie McGuire
AT RETAILERS THIS SUMMER!
Now you can get inside Lizzie's head with great new products!
JOURNALS
FRAMES
ACCESSORIES
DOLLS
Everyone loves to get applause
Watch it on
Disney Channel
abc Kids